The Peacekeeper Chronicles:

Saving Veya

Shyrel McKinley

—

Dedication

First of all I want to thank everyone who ever believed that this was possible, that I had a story to tell and the ability to tell it. I want to dedicate this book to my husband and children. Timothy has always been my biggest supporter no matter what I want to do. Even if it sounds crazy, he will always back me up and lovingly push me to pursue my dreams. My children are truly my biggest motivation to do great things with my life. I want them to know that no dream is too big and that any dream they have was God given for a purpose. Ayden and Brena were so inspirational to writing this book. Thank you for believing in me and loving me. I am also so grateful to my sister, my mom and the friends who were there to help see this thing through and offer their input. Without all of you, this dream of mine would not be here in print to share with the world. Love you all.

Prologue

Sarah woke from a fitful sleep by the sound of the phone ringing next to the bed. She never slept well during thunderstorms like this. She reached for the phone on the table next to the bed as she glanced at the clock confused that it was barely 2:00 a.m. As she answered the phone, she didn't realize that this was the call that would change her future. This phone call in the middle of the night would completely change everything for her family.

Sarah sat with her husband Cooper at the table nearly an hour after she was woken by the phone. The petite woman smoothed her auburn hair out of her face and placed her head in her hands. She was clearly distressed as he tried to make sense of the situation with her.

"We knew that one day they would ask us for help," Cooper reasoned.

His dark gray eyes stared at her with love and compassion. He knew that this was not an easy task that had been assigned to them, but one that he took with a great sense of responsibility. He tried to be delicate with his wife while expressing the importance of these next steps.

"Well yes, but I didn't expect for them to ask us to do this. Did you?" Sarah watched her husband as he got up from the table and poured another cup of coffee. She was too anxious and didn't think the coffee would help her.

"Sarah, it will be okay. Just think of the difference we will be making. And how great will it be to be parents?" Cooper smiled as he squeezed Sarah's small shoulders trying and failing to get her to relax.

Sarah led a very full life already without being a mother. Parenthood just wasn't meant for them. Although they had wanted children years before, she had given up that hope and turned her focus on running her bookstore. The idea of being a mother now to two small children was appealing to her, but there was so much she just didn't know or understand. The situation they were in was a bit different from the normal adoption or fostering of a child. It was likely to be very challenging for them. Cooper knew that, but he was forever the optimist. That's why she loved him so much.

Sarah sat in silence as Cooper finished his second cup of coffee and set out to prepare for the children to arrive. There was so much to do in just a few hours. While Cooper prepared the house, Sarah prepared her heart.

Cooper moved his weights and workout equipment from one of the spare bedrooms to the basement. They replaced the twin bed in the spare room with a toddler bed and Mickey Mouse bedding they had found. And the empty room next to theirs where he used to spend so much time lifting weights was transformed quickly into a nursery with a beautiful white crib and pink bedding. Sarah reached out to her friends for help in getting additional things they would need, and they came through in a big way. Soon their home was filled with gently used baby toys, baby seats, bottles, stuffed animals, pacifiers, jumpers, walkers, and baby gates. The sun was setting on their little cul de sac while Cooper installed two car seats into the back of Sarah's small sedan.

"I think we might need a bigger car," he said. Sarah shook her head, not quite ready to give up her car for a minivan.

Cooper and Sarah drove together down toward the river where they were to meet a man they didn't know. Cooper pulled the car up in front of an empty building in a part of town that had mostly been forgotten. They sat with the car running waiting for the stranger they were supposed to meet. Cooper held Sarah's hand to remind her that they were in this together. No matter how difficult things were going to be, he was right here. She appreciated the small gesture, but she still could not relax. The two minutes they spent waiting felt like an eternity. But then a man appeared. He literally just appeared almost as if by magic.

2

The man wore a big hat that covered most of his face and a dark blazer jacket. He carried a baby in one arm and held the hand of a small boy.

As soon as Sarah saw them standing there, she jumped out of the car. She didn't hesitate to run to the children and scoop them up into her arms. They were hers now and she felt it. She didn't know it yet, but the two tiny children would one day be the light of her life. She would do anything for them.

In a place far away a mother cried for her lost babies. She knew they were making the best decision for them, but it didn't make it easier to say goodbye. There was so much uncertainty. She was uncertain about their safety if they stayed with her. She was uncertain when she would see them again or if she would see them again. Evil was lurking and waiting to take them. She felt this was the only way she could keep them safe. The tears stained her cheeks as she sat waiting for the transporter to return. She needed to hear from him that they were safely delivered to their new home. She imagined the life they would have in this new home. It was hard to think of them living without her, but this was the decision they had made. No matter how hard it was, it was her responsibility to do what was best for them.

The transporter entered the room quietly. He didn't want to interrupt her in her time of grief.

"Everything went as planned." He spoke quietly with his head bowed low.

She nodded as she wiped the tears from her eyes and he left just as silently as he entered. She picked up a tiny blanket from the crib she was still standing in front of and held it close to her chest breathing in the scent of her baby.

Chapter One: Detention is For Suckers

Melody rushed to her class just before the bell rang. She took her seat, frazzled and out of breath, and wiped the sweat off of her brow. She couldn't believe how her day was going. It was only the second week of junior high school and every day last week had started pretty awful between finding classes, forgetting a locker combination, losing notebooks and being late. She didn't like being in a new school without her older brother who was now in his first year of high school. But Melody was determined to start this week off better somehow.

"Okay, class! Get out a pencil and put away your books. It's time for a pop quiz." Mrs. Clark instructed.

Everyone groaned and Melody thought, "Could this day get any worse?" As Melody prepared to take the pop quiz Mrs. Clark handed out to the class, she suddenly felt her skin become very warm. She thought she might be getting a fever as she felt her body get hotter and hotter. Her ears were burning and began to ring as she pulled her thick, dark blond hair into a ponytail in an attempt to cool down. She wiped her sweaty palms on her shorts. Melody started to panic as she thought she might pass out or be sick or both right here in the middle of Algebra. She fanned her face with her hands and did her best to not show her distress to the rest of the class. Out of nowhere, the ringing in her ears turned into the sound of voices. Lots of voices were coming in all at once. She couldn't understand what they were saying and the words were all jumbled up. Melody covered her ears as the voices got louder, but it did nothing to shut out all the noise.

"What's happening?" She yelled over the sound of the voices in her head. Still, with her hands over her ears, she got up from her seat and looked around the room. Everyone was staring at her like she had grown a third head.

"Don't you hear that?" Melody said to Alissa Cooley in the first row and then looked at Mrs. Clark and the rest of the class.

No one seemed bothered by all the noise.

"Melody, are you okay?" Travis Montgomery, sitting next to her, asked. Travis had always been nice and he looked genuinely concerned for Melody.

"I can't... What is that? I... I..." Melody tried to explain herself but couldn't concentrate on her words with all the noise in her head.

Her hazel eyes darted around the room frantically trying to find the source of all the noise. Did no one else hear it? And just as quickly as all of this started, it stopped. Suddenly, everything was silent again. Melody pulled her hands off of her ears hesitantly and glanced around the room again. Everyone stared back at her as she tried to compose herself. It was clear to her that she was the only one that had been affected by all the noise. No one even heard the voices. Her first thought was she had lost her mind. Terrified and embarrassed, she returned to her desk and picked up her tye dye book bag before quickly leaving the classroom.

"Melody, where are you going? Are you okay?"

Mrs. Clark followed her out into the hallway but Melody did not slow down. She power walked and then ran down the hallway and out of the school. Once Melody was in front of the school she stopped to catch her breath. "What just happened" was her first thought, followed quickly by, "What am I going to do now". Did she really just have a serious mental break in the middle of a pop quiz in Algebra class and then run out of the school in the middle of the day? Now what? Surely she wasn't allowed to just run out of the school whenever she wanted. Melody wasn't one to break the rules. She didn't know how to be defiant or disobedient. Melody never got detention or even reprimanded. She was always praised by her teachers for her behavior and good grades. Her parents always beamed with pride after parent-teacher conferences. Certainly, this behavior was not going to be so praiseful.

She decided to take her time walking around the school grounds to clear her head before going back to class. She slowly walked the track and watched the cars driving by. Melody wandered around trying to push the episode out of her head. She thought about just going home, but that didn't seem like a valid option. So Melody forced her feet to walk back into the school through the front doors and on to her next class. As she took her seat in the front of the room, a few students like

Alissa Cooley that had seen her freak out in Algebra looked at her strangely. Some of them whispered to each other, but she tried to ignore them. Melody took out her book and notebook and prepared to take History notes as Mr. Ringer lectured on about the Civil war.

Thankfully Melody managed to get through the class without a scene, and she pretended she was focused on taking notes until a few minutes before the bell rang. An office assistant entered the class and briefly spoke with Mr. Ringer. Mr. Ringer then turned to the class.

"Melody, you are wanted in the principal's office. Please collect your things and head up there."

As Melody gathered her things and put them back in her bag, she saw some of the students started whispering behind her again. Alissa Cooley was definitely talking about her. They weren't ready to let it go. What was she going to tell the principal about leaving Algebra in the middle of a pop quiz and not returning until her next class? Melody fought the knot in her stomach and her legs were a bit unstable as she walked down the hallway lined with lockers. She didn't know how she was going to explain what had happened to her and, she considered just leaving the school again as she walked toward the principal's office. There was the door. How easy would it be to just walk right out and not come back? Or she could tell them she had a mental breakdown, a panic attack, or something. Hopefully, they could understand that. Things like that can happen to overworked pop stars and housewives so surely they can happen to overstressed junior high girls.

Reluctantly, Melody entered the office and told the secretary that she was there to see the principal. She was instructed to wait in one of the wooden chairs that lined the office wall. She had missed her chance to run off. The principal, Mrs. Stein, was a scary woman. She was built like a linebacker with broad shoulders and a thick torso. Mrs. Stein never smiled at anyone. Kids told stories about her strict punishments and verbal assaults. Melody had hoped she would never have to actually talk to her face to face. Yet here she was on her first week of school already waiting in the principal's office. This was not exactly how she had seen her junior high school career going. She nervously twirled her hair around her finger and tried to focus on breathing slowly in order to calm her nerves. A few minutes later Mrs. Stein opened the door to her office and beckoned Melody inside.

"Hello, Miss McCarthy. I called you here to speak with you about leaving Mrs. Clark's class today." Mrs. Stein patted her curly red hair as she spoke. She sat at her large metal desk staring at Melody like she was the judge, jury, and executioner. Melody knew this wasn't going to go very well and chose her words carefully.

"I am so sorry. I think I was having a panic attack or something and I just had to get out."

"Miss McCarthy, you cannot just leave school and return as you see fit because you were not prepared for a pop quiz."

Melody's face turned red. She wished that she could explain what had happened and that it wasn't because of the quiz that she ran out of the classroom. Instead, she just nodded her head and looked down at her feet. Mrs. Stein continued to lecture her on attendance and proper etiquette for feeling ill. And Melody left the office with after-school detention. Melody couldn't believe this was actually happening to her. Melody had tarnished her perfect school record. She could just imagine her permanent record now stained with a big red "DETENTION". Her parents were going to be so disappointed in her when they found out.

"Melody, this isn't like you. Why would you just leave class?" Mom asked as soon as Melody got into the van.

Of course, the school had already notified their parents about what happened so they knew she would be in detention. Melody stared at her blue toenails in her sandaled feet and swallowed back her tears before she answered her mom.

"I...I don't know. I wasn't feeling well and should have handled it better." Melody replied.

All that time to think of an excuse and that was the best answer she could give. She just wasn't sure how to tell her the truth about what happened.

"And what about you? What do you have to say for yourself?" Mom turned her attention toward Ezra sitting in the seat next to her.

"It was an accident," Ezra answered. "I swear I don't know how it happened."

"What is she talking about, Ez," Melody leaned forward to hear him better.

"I broke a desk. No big deal, but I got detention too," Ezra shrugged.

They continued home in silence. Clearly, their mother was disappointed in them. Melody could tell by the way her mom tightly pursed her lips with both hands on the steering wheel. She avoided eye contact with Ezra who was in the seat next to her and looked like she was deep in thought. She was plotting their punishment, no doubt. Mom was usually very creative with punishments. Ezra had spent plenty of time writing essays and doing crazy household chores as punishment in the past. Melody spent the car ride thinking about what had happened. She wasn't able to explain it to herself, let alone someone else. She had tried to wrap her head around it all day, but it still made no sense to her. What was with the voices she heard? Why did they start? What made them stop? Was this going to happen to her again? She thought for sure they would lock her away in some hospital somewhere if it happened again. Maybe she was getting sick or something? Maybe it was just a fluke event?

Ezra and Melody lived with their adoptive mother and father in a cute little house on a dead end street. They had grown up knowing that they were biological siblings, but Sarah and Cooper McCarthy with their dark hair and short stature were not the biological parents to these two tall, blonde children. Ezra was two years older than Melody. Shortly after Melody was born, their parents decided it was better for them to be raised by the McCarthy's. Sarah would sometimes tell her stories about her parents and what they were like. Sarah told Melody of a beautiful queen with blonde hair and a soft voice. She often spoke of the bravest king anyone had ever seen. When Melody was small she thought the fairytales were true. She imagined a very beautiful mother who loved her very much and sang her to sleep. She thought of the brave king in a suit of armor ready to fight off any monsters. Now that she was older, she knew they were just stories that parents tell their children. Parents often made up stories with their children as royalty or mermaids. The stories Sarah told her were probably just to make a small girl feel better about being adopted. She wondered if Ezra thought about their parents as much as she did because it wasn't something that the siblings really talked about. It seemed like an insult to Sarah and Cooper to talk about their biological parents after all they had given them. It wasn't like either of them really had any memories to reminisce over anyway. Everything before moving in with the McCarthy's was blank for the both of them. Sarah and Cooper were the only mom and dad they ever knew.

Being adopted was about the extent of weird in the McCarthy children's lives. Everything else was very normal and ordinary until today's events. They had a simple two-story home and her parents both worked boring jobs, Cooper in construction and Sarah was part owner of a bookstore. Her mother drove a minivan and her father had a pickup truck. Melody did well in school and worked hard on her singing lessons. She had lots of friends at school and loved spending time on her phone or with her best friend like most 12-year-old girls. Ezra's baseball team loved him for his talent. He sometimes caused trouble at school, but for the most part, got good grades and was kind to others. He played video games and was a big movie buff for 14. The two bickered constantly like most brothers and sisters, but they also shared a great bond. Ezra was always Melody's protector. Things were as ordinary as they come in their boring town in the middle of the boring Midwest. The town they lived in felt like a small town even though there were over 20,000 people living there. It felt like everyone knew everyone. Sarah and Cooper were a big part of the community and the family went to church together every Sunday. But Melody felt like something had changed in their quiet life.

The next day began just like any other. Melody got ready for school, had breakfast, and her mom drove her to school. Nothing seemed out of the ordinary today so Melody was hopeful for a better day. She made it to class on time and was able to make up the pop quiz she missed the day before in Algebra. She joked with her friends at lunch and made plans for Friday night while trying to put the day before out of her mind. Everyone else seemed to have let it go and her friends didn't even ask about it. Mom picked Melody up from school to take her to her singing lessons and didn't seem upset with her any more. Melody was relieved to see her mom in a better mood. They talked about her plans for Friday night and how her classes were going on the drive. In fact, things seemed so normal; she even wondered if the events of the day before had really happened.

They pulled up to the music academy where Melody took singing lessons from Ms. Capechio twice a week for the last five years. The music academy was housed in a two-story brick building downtown that used to be a family home. Ms. Capechio had been a talented singer who aspired to be in Broadway musicals, but when that didn't work out, she returned home to set up her music school. They taught all kinds of music lessons at the school including singing.

As she walked up the old stairs to the second-floor music room, Melody felt her skin get hot. She started to panic. "Not again," she thought quickly putting the thought that maybe yesterday hadn't happened out of her mind. She couldn't have a total mental breakdown in front of her mentor. She didn't want anyone else thinking she was losing her mind. She paused on the stairs preparing herself for the ringing in her ears and the strange voices. Suddenly she had a sharp shooting pain in her head and a flash. Melody saw an image like a memory. It was Ms. Capechio yelling and angry. She didn't hear what she was yelling, and she couldn't remember a time where she had seen her angry at her. It was a quick flash and it was gone. Melody was left standing in the stairwell gripping the railing tight. She was just as stunned and confused as before. She wasn't sure what she had just seen. Anxiously, she took the rest of the stairs slowly and made it to the room. She was worried something else would happen in front of her teacher, but she couldn't turn back now. By the time she made it to the room, she was no longer feeling hot and pained.

There was a man she did not recognize sitting in the chair in the corner of the room. He stood up as she entered and walked toward her.

"You must be Melody," the strange man said putting out his large hand to shake.

"Yes," she smiled and took the man's hand.

"I am George Carson. I have heard so much about you."

George Carson was a tall, muscular man. He didn't look like most Broadway performers with his slightly curved back and crooked nose. His eyes were deep set and dark. Melody thought he looked a little scary and she wondered what he was doing in Ms. Capechio's room when she was supposed to have her lesson. George explained that Ms. Capechio had a family emergency and would be out of town for a few weeks. She had asked him to fill in for her because she did not want her students to miss out on their lessons. He told her that he was happy to fill in because he loved teaching. Mr. George Carson went on to list his singing achievements and education probably because he could tell that Melody was skeptical.

"I know you were currently working on 'On the Steps of the Palace'. Should we go ahead and get started?" Mr. Carson walked over to the piano in the middle of the room and Melody took her place next to him to begin.

He played a couple of notes so Melody could get her voice warmed up first. She felt uncomfortable singing with the stranger since she had not fully conquered her stage fright, but tried her best to concentrate on the music. After the events of the day before, Melody needed the time with her music. Music always brought her so much peace, but she was having difficulty getting into it for some reason. Mr. Carson continued playing as Melody sang through the song. Melody glanced at him out of the corner of her eye as he was playing. Her breath caught in her throat when she swore she saw his beady eyes glowing yellow like a wild animal in the dark. He looked at her when she missed a beat, and the glow was gone.

"I think my mom is probably here," Melody said quickly as she pretended to check her phone. Her mom hadn't called and she still had another twenty minutes in her lesson. But something did not feel right about this. She didn't feel comfortable being alone with this man a second longer.

"Are you sure? We still have time to practice," George said in a terse voice.

He seemed agitated, but smiled anyway and told her it was so nice to work with her, and he would see her for the next lesson later in the week. Melody left the school as fast as she could and started down the street. She wasn't sure what she was going to do for the next twenty minutes while she waited for her mom to pick her up, but she didn't want to run into Mr. Carson outside of the music academy. Melody used her iPhone to look up "glowing eyes" while she waited for her mom around the block. She wasn't able to find an explanation for what she knew she saw in the music room before she had to meet her mom back at the music academy.

When Sarah pulled up in front of the academy, Melody was waiting on the curb on full alert. She glanced around to be sure George Carson wasn't around as she climbed into the van. She almost let out a sigh of relief as the car pulled away from the school. Melody wondered what her mom would say if she told her what she saw. It certainly wasn't normal, and her mom was not going to have an explanation either, she was sure of it. And she was also sure she wasn't going to go back to singing lessons until Ms. Capechio returned from her trip.

"You seem awfully quiet. How was your lesson?" Mom asked.

"It was fine. Ms. Capechio is away because of some family emergency. Another teacher filled in, but there won't be lessons again until she returns in a couple weeks." Melody lied.

12

Melody couldn't remember ever lying to her mom before, and she didn't feel good about lying to her now. It was worth it not to have to be alone with that creep again, she thought.

Chapter Two: Fastballs and Alien Theories

Ezra woke up late again. As he rushed around his room looking for something clean to wear his eyes wandered over the small gold box sitting on his dresser. The little golden gift box he recently received that was just taking up space and collecting dust, but he dreamed about the feather-light golden chain and its small golden charm every night for the past week. This necklace was a gift from his parents along with a similar chain for Melody. His parents told them that the necklaces were the only thing they had from their life before being adopted. They both wore the chains with their small disc-shaped charms around their necks. Each charm was unique with intricate designs engraved into the gold. Ezra had never been a fan of wearing jewelry but there was something different about this necklace. He couldn't describe the pull that it had on him. He just really desired to have it with him at all times. After throwing on some clothes that seemed clean enough, he glanced in the dirty mirror above his dresser and combed his fingers through his blonde hair. Then grabbed his book bag and hurried downstairs where his mom was waiting to take him and Melody to school.

"About time, mister," Mom said impatiently as they hurried out the door.

"Try not to get into trouble today," Mom told them both as they got out of the car at school obviously not forgetting the detention from the day before.

"Yeah, yeah," Ezra replied rolling his eyes with his back to his mom.

As he walked up to school, he repeated the sentence to himself. "Try not to get into trouble today."

Ezra didn't even make it through first period before strange things started happening again. He thought he was losing his mind, but he felt like he had to hold himself back so that he didn't accidentally break something. Everything seemed so fragile in his hands recently. Ezra almost pulled the classroom door off the hinges when he opened it. He hoped no one had noticed. Looking around quickly, it seemed like the coast was clear. He carefully sat in his desk and cautiously set his books on top of the desk afraid everything might crumble under him.

Ezra repeated these careful steps in every class throughout the day. He practically tiptoed down the hallways taking extra precautions so that he wouldn't bump into anyone because he was fearful he would actually cause them harm. Even with all this extreme caution he still broke a pencil trying to take notes in second period. His shoestring broke as he was trying to tie his new shoes in P.E.

However, baseball practice was a different story. Ezra's heart was racing and he felt a knot in his stomach as he prepared for practice with stretches on the field. When his best friend, David, asked him to warm up his arm with him he declined worried that he wouldn't be in control and might hurt another teammate or even his best friend. The first 30 minutes of practice went smoothly. He was able to stay at the back of the batting lineup and hang out in the outfield without anyone noticing. Ezra couldn't remember a time where he had been at practice and not touched the baseball. It was probably better that way, he thought. With just a few minutes left of the practice, Coach Thompson asked Ezra to pitch.

"You know Coach, I'm not really feeling it today," Ezra tried to get out of pitching. "Let Miller get the extra practice."

"Come on Ezra, we have our tournament this weekend and we need you ready!" Coach was not going to take no for an answer.

Ezra reluctantly stood on the pitcher's mound. He did a quick practice wind up and took a deep breath. David was up to bat. The last thing Ezra wanted to do was nail his best friend with the fastest fastball of his life. He thought, "Easy does it" over and over in his head before he released the pitch. The fastest pitch any of them had ever seen. It flew by David's head and hit the chain link fence with so much force that it broke through the fence.

"Whoa!" Coach looked at Ezra and back at the fence.

The rest of the team stood slack-jawed staring at Ezra. Ezra wished he could just disappear right then and there. His face turned bright red and he went to the dugout to hide while the coach walked over to inspect the fence. Ezra buried his head in his glove as the rest of the team came running in.

"How'd you do that?"

"What happened?"

"Did you really just throw that through the fence?"

"I've never seen a pitch that fast!"

The dugout was full of loud voices all at once questioning Ezra. He didn't have an answer. How was he supposed to explain what just happened to them? His head was spinning. He wasn't going to be able to think with all these voices around that was for sure. So he gathered up his things and ran out of the dugout, leaving the noise behind him. Ezra ran and ran and ran but didn't seem to get tired or out of breath. His first thought was to keep running until he just couldn't any more, but he wasn't winding down at all. The wind blew through his hair as he continued to gain speed. He ran all the way across town past the high school and all the stores with his baseball bag on his back and headed for the bike trails that would take him through the woods. Ezra's legs didn't stop until he was deep into the woods and all alone. He wiped the sweat off of his forehead with the back of his hand and sat down right in the middle of the dirt trail.

"What is happening to me!?" He yelled into the empty woods.

Ezra continued to sit in the woods until it began to get dark. By now his mom would have went to pick him up from practice. She would know what happened. Would she be mad at him or would she be worried? Ezra decided to dig his phone out of his bag and see if she had tried to call him. Sure enough, he had 12 missed calls from his mom and seven from his dad. Melody had also sent him multiple text messages. He decided it might be best to read Melody's messages first so he had an idea of how Mom was behaving first.

Melody: Where are you?

Mom is looking for you

You left practice? What happened?

Everyone is saying something crazy happened at practice and you took off!

Mom is freaking out! She is so scared!

Answer me! Now I am getting scared!

Ezra: I'm fine. I can't really explain what happened and I'm scared to come home.

Melody: Just come home.

After Ezra read Melody's last message, he decided it was time to get home and face his parents. He ran home as fast as he could in the dark. His dad's truck wasn't in the driveway when he got there. He forced his long legs up the front porch steps and tried to prepare himself for what might be on the other side of the door.

Mom was in the kitchen on the phone as Ezra walked in. She saw him and dropped the phone. Sarah grabbed her boy into a big hug and started to cry.

"I was so worried about you! Don't you ever do that to me again!"

After what seemed like a few minutes of being held by his mom, she let go and picked the phone back up.

"Cooper, he's home," She said into the phone and dad ended his search and returned home.

The next day, Ezra didn't want to get out of bed in the morning. He spent most of the night awake, tossing and turning in his bed. He couldn't explain what happened to anyone and wanted to hide out in his room. When he didn't get out of bed in the morning, Sarah came into his room and said she would call the school, and he could stay in bed. Before she left for work, she came in to check on him but didn't bring up the events of the night before. It wasn't like her to not try to pry for information or want an explanation. Sarah took her responsibility as a mother seriously and always wanted to know what was going on in her children's lives. She also didn't let them get away with much. But today, she kissed him on his forehead and just left for the day. Her eyes said she was worried, but she didn't say a word. Ezra wasn't sure why she avoided talking about what happened, but he didn't want to talk about it either.

After catching up on sleep, Ezra decided that although he was embarrassed by the things that were happening, maybe it wasn't so bad after all. He wondered if he could duplicate the pitch from the day before and what else he might be able to do. He decided to test it. He quickly showered and checked the time. He still had a couple of hours before his mom would be home from work with Melody from school. He grabbed a baseball from his bag and went into the back yard.

Ezra started by practicing his pitching. Sure enough, he was able to throw the ball at a speed he had never seen before, not even in the major leagues. He could run faster than any human that he had ever seen and even after an hour of throwing the ball and running after it, he wasn't tired at all. He thought he would try out some new things. So Ezra made his way to his dad's workout area in the basement. He began lifting weights. He started out small and quickly realized that he could lift much more than what was available to him here in the basement. "Whoa!" He thought for sure this must be a world record for lifting from a 14-year-old boy!

Ezra remembered all the superhero movies and started to think that it was possible he was an alien from some far away planet like Superman or was it possible he was bitten by a radioactive spider like Spiderman. There didn't seem to be any other logical explanation for the strange super strength appearing out of nowhere.

Later that night, Ezra helped Melody clear the dinner plates from the table in silence. Mom and dad were still pretty upset about Ezra disappearing, and no one was talking about what happened at baseball practice. That day someone from the music academy had also called mom and told her that Melody had missed her lesson. The teacher explained that her usual teacher was away, but the substitute had been expecting Melody. Mom was upset that Melody lied about not having lessons and wasted the instructor's time waiting for her. Ezra felt bad for Melody. She didn't usually get in trouble, and something was definitely up with her. He wondered if he should find some time to talk to her when mom and dad weren't around and try to figure out what was going on with her.

"Melody, will you help me with the dishes?" He asked.

But he could tell she just wanted to get away as quick as she could. She must be pretty freaked out. What would cause his usually happy, well-behaved sister to get a detention and lie to their mom all in the same week? Ezra wanted to tell her how he broke the desk and the new abilities he had discovered. He hadn't handled things well after baseball practice, but now he was excited to tell someone. He knew he could trust Melody.

"I think that we should talk," Ezra whispered to Melody as they cleared the plates.

She looked at him strangely because she knew something was up, but she agreed with a silent nod of her head. Once they were out of their parents' sight, Melody began to tell Ezra what had really happened during Algebra class. By the time she finished explaining the incident in the music room, she was in tears. Ezra awkwardly patted her back. He wasn't much for hugs and that kind of thing, but he didn't like when his sister was upset.

"It's okay, Melody. Something really strange has been happening to me too."

"Really? What happened?" Melody looked at him and wiped her eyes.

"I don't know what is going on, but I seriously just bumped into that desk and it fell to the floor in pieces. How crazy is that? Who would believe that? Melody, I think I have like super strength!"

Melody smiled and covered her mouth to keep in a laugh. But she didn't say anything. Neither of them spoke for what seemed like forever. They silently finished up the dishes before either of them spoke again, each of them thinking deeply about what the other had shared.

"Should we tell mom and dad?" Melody asked.

"Who is going to believe us?" Ezra replied.

"They are our parents. Come on, Ezra. It's not like they are going to have us locked away or something. They have to believe us," Melody reasoned.

"You are awfully optimistic."

Ezra was terrified to have to tell them. He convinced Melody to wait while they tried to sort it out on their own. Although Sarah and Cooper had always treated them with love, being adopted did make him fear that something like this could change everything. Was their bond really the same as it would be with their own biological children?

"I think I need to see this super strength," Melody laughed.

"We should probably try to figure out what is up with that singing instructor," Ezra replied seriously.

He was worried about his sister having to go back to lessons with George Carson. Ezra and Melody went to Ezra's room to use the computer. They decided to see if they could find anything out about George Carson on the internet. He had claimed to have many singing achievements, but with a quick Google search, they were not able to find anything on George Carson.

19

"What do you think this means?" Melody asked Ezra as he was scanning through the search results again.

"I can't find anything on him. I think it means he is not who he says he is, Melody."

"Then who is he?" Melody wasn't sure what they were supposed to do with this information. "And what about his glowing eyes?"

"Maybe he's some kind of alien. Maybe we are aliens too!" Ezra seemed excited at this possibility. Melody was not.

"Aliens? Really? That is your explanation for all of this weirdness?" She retorted. "You can't possibly believe that we are aliens and that after all these years we are just now going to find that out and if so, how would some random substitute teacher show up and also be an alien?" She shook her head as she walked out of his room.

As Melody left Ezra's room he couldn't stop thinking about this theory. He started to search for any theories about aliens and superhumans that he could find online until his mom interrupted him with a knock at the door.

"Ezra, did you finish your homework?" She poked her head into his room as he quickly closed his laptop that was sitting on the desk so she couldn't see that he was reading about aliens.

"No mom, but I will get right on that," he replied as he closed the door on her.

Homework was going to have to wait, Ezra decided. Finding out who he really was had to come first. If he was an alien, school wouldn't matter that much anyway. He continued reading articles claiming to be scientific studies and all kinds of conspiracy theories until his mom said it was lights out. He waited a good 20 minutes before quietly starting his search again in the dark bedroom hidden under the covers with his phone. Ezra realized quickly that he wouldn't be getting any sleep.

.

Chapter Three: A Nightmare of a Dinner

Melody stood in a beautiful meadow. She could smell the flowers on the gentle breeze as she followed her brother through the tall grass. The colors were bold and vibrant even in her dreams. She had never seen such beautiful greens and purples before. They were walking towards a hillside dotted with purple and red trees. Melody was having trouble keeping up with Ezra while she admired all the beautiful things around her. The giant butterflies, hummingbirds, and other insects all seemed brand new. And they all flew around her like they wanted to say hello. Melody felt the meadow calming her it was overwhelmingly tranquil. To the left, there were far away mountain peaks. To the right forests went as far as she could see. Melody was certain that there was no place like this meadow in the entire world.

Melody woke up feeling relaxed after dreaming of the most peaceful meadow again that night. Today was a milestone day for her and she had a lot to look forward to as a perfectly normal 12-year-old girl with her friends. Now that she was in junior high, mom and dad had agreed to let her go to the high school sports games with her friends unsupervised. Tonight was the big homecoming game, and she would finally get a taste of freedom. After the craziness of the week, Melody wanted to feel like a normal kid. She wanted to hang out with her friends pretending to care about the game, but really socializing was the priority. She wanted to eat popcorn and talk about boys like nothing was out of the ordinary. She quickly got dressed in her favorite red and white Panthers shirt to support the high school team and was ready for school. Melody grabbed her books and hoped she would have time to finish up the homework she had been neglecting in study hall that morning.

"Did you get any sleep?" Melody asked Ezra when she saw him with his head on the kitchen table.

He didn't even bother to look up at her as he groaned in response. His blonde hair was disheveled and he wore a wrinkled t-shirt with his jeans.

"What is the matter with him?" Dad asked as he came into the kitchen to grab his coffee on his way out the door to his construction job site.

"I don't think he has been sleeping well," Mom said. She kissed dad good-bye and went about making her own coffee. Melody sensed that mom was concerned but she didn't say any more.

"Don't forget about the homecoming game tonight," Melody reminded her dad before he left. He had promised to give her and her friends a ride to the game.

The day flew by without anything strange happening. Melody rushed to meet her mom at the pickup line and was already texting her friend Nora about the game on the way home from school. Nora was coming to Melody's house at 5:00 so they could ride to the game together. Nora had been Melody's best friend since 2nd grade. They had grown up a block away from each other, and their friendship started over a mutual love of My Little Ponies in Mrs. Elm's class. Like them, it had grown and matured over the years. Now they had a mutual love for Justin Bieber and the new kid, Liam Jensen.

By ten after 5:00, Melody and Nora were getting ready for the game together. Melody shared her makeup with her friend as they talked about who else would be at the football game.

"So do you think Liam will be there?" Nora asked Melody.

"I heard him talking with Jaxon in science class about going together!" Melody was excited to relay the information to her friend.

"Oh, Liam! I love you!" Ezra stuck his head in the door to mock the girls when he overheard their conversation.

"Get out of here!" Melody yelled at him and slammed the door in his face. He was always picking on her in front of her friends to try to make himself look cool. Sometimes she hated having an older brother.

Nora used the mirror at Melody's vanity to fix her shaggy bangs and run a brush through her short brown hair. Melody and Nora had not been alone together since everything was going crazy. She looked at Nora and wished she could tell her what had been happening. But what would she tell her? She wasn't sure if she should keep it between her and Ezra. Melody had always been able to tell Nora everything. She didn't think that had changed. She didn't want to waste the night thinking about it all, but it would be nice to be able to talk about it.

Cooper drove the girls to the game and told Melody he would be back to pick them up later. The girls got out of the car and quickly headed inside the stadium. They gathered with their friends in the bleachers. Melody had butterflies in her stomach as she sat on the bleachers with her friends. Being at the game without her parents was a big deal. But she was also nervous that something strange might happen and ruin it all. Being a preteen was hard enough without the possibility of being an alien.

It was nice to feel like any other ordinary kid again with everyone around her at the game. Wearing her red and black spirit sweatshirt, she looked just like the rest of the kids in the crowd. It was easy to feel a little normal as she blended in. They didn't watch much of the game as everyone sat around gossiping about teachers, the boys they liked, and the girls that they didn't. During half time Melody asked Nora to go with her to get popcorn. As they walked across the bleachers toward the concessions, Melody had a strange feeling like she was being watched. Then the hot flashes began. Melody felt hot and sweaty. The ringing in her ears hit her hard. She couldn't hear the crowd over it. Melody felt dizzy and reached for Nora as she quickly took a seat on a bleacher next to her before she fell over.

"Are you okay?" Nora asked, but Melody didn't hear her.

Nora's face was wrinkled in worry. Melody put her hands over her ears to try to block out all the noise. And then she could hear the voices. They came in all at once. Melody tried to steady her thoughts and focus on breathing. She still felt dizzy and didn't think she could stand up, but felt the need to get out of there. As she looked around the audience she noticed him. Mr. Carson was sitting in the bleachers not 10 feet away. He stared back at her. Now she really needed to get away.

"Can you help me get out of here?" she asked Nora and didn't wait for her to answer before taking her arm and trying to stand slowly.

Nora led Melody out of the stadium and into the parking lot where it was quiet before Melody stopped walking.

"What's going on?" Nora asked.

By the time they made it to the parking lot, Melody had finally collected herself. She had to tell Nora what was going on. She explained the hot flash, dizziness, ringing in her ears, and the sound of voices in her head. Melody told Nora about Ezra's theories and even about the singing instructor. "Wow! Why didn't you tell me?" Nora asked. She seemed like she was genuinely worried about Melody. Melody was so relieved to finally tell someone. Nora really seemed to believe her. Nora hugged her and told her that she was there for her and she didn't want her to feel alone.

The girls spent the rest of the game anxiously waiting for Cooper to pick them back up. Nora helped Melody keep an eye on the lot to make sure Mr. Carson didn't show up. Melody was certain he was there watching her, and he scared her more than the strange voices she kept hearing.

Melody was sitting in her dining room at the table with her family. Ezra looked at her and grabbed her hand when suddenly the lights went out. Her father got up from the table to investigate as the whole house began to shake like they were in an earthquake. Melody let out a small scream, and she grabbed ahold of the table to steady herself. The house began to shake harder, and she could hear things falling off the walls crashing to the floor.

"Dad, where are you?" Ezra yelled out.

Melody couldn't see anything other than the dark objects that were Ezra and Sarah at the table next to her. Ezra got up to look around. Melody tried to stop him by placing her hand on his arm, but he left the room in the direction their father had gone moments before. Things started falling everywhere around her, and she thought the roof was caving in. Melody screamed.

Melody woke with a start! She sat up in bed drenched in sweat. It was still dark outside her bedroom window when she climbed out of bed and went to the bathroom. She splashed cold water on her face and told herself it was just a bad dream. Everything was okay because her family was safe. Melody was sure she wouldn't be able to fall back to sleep after that terrifying dream. It had felt more real than any dream she had before. So she went to her desk and turned on her computer. Melody tried to study for a test for Monday, but she was having a difficult time focusing. With everything going on with her and Ezra the last week, she found that school didn't matter as much. Instead of studying, she searched for articles about people with super strength.

Melody spent what felt like hours searching and managed to come up with a few articles claiming to be real, but she didn't know if she could believe any of the sources. She decided to call it quits when the sun finally came up. She showered and took her time getting ready since it was the weekend. Melody brushed and dried her hair. She wasn't allowed to wear much makeup but she liked to wear a little pale purple eye shadow and mascara because she liked the way it made her hazel eyes look. Melody walked down the hallway past Ezra's closed bedroom door and downstairs to get breakfast. She sat in silence at the table eating her chocolatey cereal while thoughts of superhumans, aliens, and shaking rooms swam in her head. Her mind was filled with chaos as she tried and failed to shake the dream.

Ezra came down the stairs as Melody was sitting at the table staring off into space. He didn't seem bothered at all this morning and actually looked like he was in a good mood, Melody thought.

"How long have you been sitting here?" Ezra asked as he looked at Melody's soggy bowl of cereal sitting on the table in front of her. She had barely touched it.

"I'm not sure," She shrugged. Melody got up from the table and dumped the bowl in the sink as Ezra made himself some cereal.

"You don't look so hot, sis," Ezra said before shoving a spoonful of cereal into his mouth.

Melody went on to tell Ezra what happened at the football game the night before.

"How am I going to go back to singing lessons next week? What if I hear voices again? This may be all fun and games for you Ezra, but I am terrified." Melody whispered angrily at her brother and backed out of the kitchen.

She was right, Ezra thought to himself as he sat in the kitchen alone. He had to try to find a way to get her out of singing lessons so she would feel better. He wanted to protect his sister, but he wasn't sure where to start. After he finished his breakfast, Ezra found Melody in her room. He wanted her to know he was sorry and that he was going to keep her safe. They needed to work together because he was going to need her help too.

"You were right. I am sorry. I promise I am going to help you. We will figure this all out," He tried to make her feel better.

"Did you find anything helpful yet?" Melody asked as she patted her bed for Ezra to sit down next to her.

He grabbed her laptop off the desk and showed her a few articles he found interesting, but none of it seemed to relate to them. Melody could see Ezra's excitement in his blue eyes as he read an article about aliens to her.

"Do you really think you are an alien?" Melody asked skeptically.

"Maybe we both are. Or some other kind of superhuman! You never know! I don't want to rule anything out."

While the two kids sat on the bed reading articles, they heard their parents get up and go downstairs. Dad headed to the gym like he did most weekend mornings, and their mom went outside to work in the yard. With their parents distracted, Melody wanted to see what Ezra could do.

Ezra took turns lifting different pieces of furniture in Melody's room with ease. And then it occurred to him. "What if you hearing voices in your head were really something else?"

Melody didn't understand at first. She looked at him quizzically and he continued, "Melody, what if you were hearing everyone's thoughts!"

"Then why did it stop?" She thought out loud, "Or why did it start for that matter?"

"Maybe you just don't know how to control it yet. And maybe something triggered it." Ezra went to the window and looked outside as he tried to think of what could trigger all of this to begin. How did they suddenly have some kind of superhuman abilities? Is that what this was? Ezra was excited that maybe he had found the answer! But Melody still wasn't sure. It seemed crazy but she didn't have any other explanation.

As Ezra was deep in thought still, something caught his eye. It was the small golden box on Melody's desk. It was identical to the box that he had in his room. The charms that came from these matching boxes were unique. Each charm was a small golden disc engraved and carved with different emblems. Every year, they celebrated a special holiday for adoptive families. They called it their "gotcha day". This was the day that Ezra and Melody were adopted by Sarah and Cooper. They had celebrated this day two weeks ago. Sarah and Cooper decided that it was time to give them these boxes which were actually Ezra and Melody's only possessions when they were brought to them in the middle of the night 10 years ago.

"What about these? They are kinda strange and unusual. Maybe they are some kind of trigger?" Ezra asked picking up the box from Melody's shelf and looking it over.

They hadn't really talked about the boxes or received much of an explanation. The only thing they knew about the golden boxes was that they had come from their birth parents. Melody just shrugged taking the box from him and placing back on the shelf. But Ezra felt there was something more to these boxes and the necklaces that came inside. He thought he felt something when he picked up the box. He couldn't quite describe the feeling, but it was like the box had its own energy or force.

"Ezra, we need to figure out how we are going to deal with Mr. Carson and keep these strange things to ourselves. Focus," Melody said completely forgetting about the golden box.

Before dad got home from the gym, they had decided that Ezra would go with her to singing lessons next time so he could check out the substitute instructor himself. Then they would go from there. Until then, they were going to try to hide Ezra's super strength. Melody wasn't sure how she was going to keep people from seeing her lose it again if in fact, this was some sort of special power she had just gained, but she would have to worry about that later. They didn't want to risk mom and dad hearing anything. So Ezra returned to his room to play video games on his computer and Melody made plans with her friends just like any normal Saturday.

Sunday was the big championship baseball game Ezra and his team had been preparing for. He had tried to think of ways to get out of going and failed. His mom didn't believe he was sick and his dad pushed him to go anyway.

"You know how important this is to your team. You made a commitment and I think you need to hold up your end, Ez," his dad lectured.

"I know all that and I want to help the team, but I really think I am sick. Something was going around school last week," Ezra pleaded.

No luck! The family drove together to the baseball game in Sarah's minivan. Ezra sat sulking in the backseat next to Melody. There was no way he was going to be able to play the game without something happening like last time. Melody tried to reassure him. She believed in him and thought he would be able to control it if he really tried. Dad was right, the team was counting on him and if he didn't show everyone would be asking a million questions. Ezra had done his best to avoid all the questions as it was by playing it cool. Everyone thought it was just some crazy amount of talent which only made them

27

need him for this game even more. Ezra had considered telling his coach he was on steroids even just to explain the strange amount of strength he had developed and to get him out of the game.

Melody sat with her friends in the bleachers cheering on her brother. She could feel his anxiety as he stepped up to bat. She was sweating and sick to her stomach for him. Everyone was watching with anticipation. The baseball coach was excited to see what Ezra could do after his fastpitch had gone through the fence at practice. He was sure that Ezra was their new secret weapon for winning this tournament for the first year in a long time. It was unusual for a freshman to have so much talent which drew everyone's attention.

The pitcher stepped into position and readied his pitch. The ball left the pitcher's hand and flew toward Ezra. Ezra took deep breaths focusing every bit of himself on self-control. For once he was actually terrified of that ball. How ironic that he had never been scared to play baseball before now. And now he could do incredible things if he wanted to. But he didn't want to, not with the crowd of people that could be hurt if things didn't go his way. Ezra bunted the ball as it came across the plate in front of him. When it made impact with the bat, the ball soared high into the air and straight over the fence. Ezra got the first home run of the season with a little bunt. The crowd went wild. The players ran the bases while the other team stood there confused. The players in the outfield were left scratching their heads because clearly, that ball should not have gone over that fence. He made it look so easy as he ran the bases with his hands in the air. He even took a bow at home plate.

Melody couldn't help but laugh at her brother's lack of modesty. Of course, he would take the opportunity to show off. But she was proud of the way he managed to control his strength under all of that pressure. If he could learn to do that, then maybe she could have some kind of control over the voices she had been hearing.

The rest of the game went just as smoothly. Ezra made giant strides in learning self-control during that game. But everyone was still wondering how he managed to get home runs so easily. And his fastballs were record-breaking.

"We are going to have to get some college scouts out here to watch you boy! And that's not something we usually do with freshman," Coach Thompson raved over Ezra's game-winning plays all day.

On Monday, Ezra did his best to keep his new found super strength hidden. He was careful and avoided making a scene and detention. After winning the baseball championship for the first time in years, everyone was talking to him suddenly and although he would normally love the spotlight, it made it more difficult to hide the fact that one day last week he woke up with some kind of super strength. Melody managed to get through the school day without anything unusual happening.

On Tuesday afternoon Ezra was headed to singing lessons with Melody. She could tell that mom thought it was strange Ezra was tagging along, but she didn't question them about it. Maybe she was glad they were spending time together when they didn't always get along, but things did seem different with mom ever since Ezra pitched a baseball through a fence and disappeared. Mom seemed to be giving him extra space like she didn't know what to say to him.

Ezra followed as Melody led the way up the stairs and to the music room where George Carson was waiting to begin lessons. Everything started out just like it had before. Melody warmed up with George playing the piano. She felt very uncomfortable with Mr. Carson, but she didn't think he was an alien, as Ezra had suggested. However, she did not want him to know just how uncomfortable she felt, because he frightened her. They ran through her song for the concert once before Mr. Carson asked if she would like to take a short break.

"I think it is great that your parents are so invested in your singing," Mr. Carson said.

Melody just nodded in response. He was trying to make small talk but Melody didn't want to chat with him. Ezra sat in the corner of the room so that he was not a distraction, but he had a clear view of Mr. Carson. He stared at those beady eyes but so far he did not see anything out of the ordinary. He felt that something was off about this guy, but he just couldn't figure out what it was as he stared at him playing the piano while Melody sang along.

"You two are lucky to be adopted by the same family, yes?" George asked gesturing toward Ezra with a nod.

Melody was caught off guard. How did he know they were adopted? Or that they were lucky to be with the same family, as in he knew they were biological siblings adopted together? Melody looked at Ezra in shock. She didn't know what she should say or do next. Ezra walked toward where they sat in the middle of the room.

"I'm sorry, Mr. Carson, is it? I don't know why that is any of your business," he replied.

By the look on George's face, it was clear he had slipped up and given something away. He knew about them, and now they knew it. And there it was, a quick flash of glowing yellow eyes. Ezra grabbed Melody's hand.

"We're leaving," he said matter of factly as Melody followed him out the door.

"Stop!" George yelled.

Ezra started walking faster as they went down the stairs and out on to the street. George was still following them. Melody was having a hard time keeping up as Ezra practically dragged her down the street. But George was still behind them yelling.

"He's keeping up," Ezra said as he quickly scooped Melody up on his back and started to run.

Ezra ran at full speed down the street and out of the neighborhood. His long legs ran as fast as they could across town dodging cars and other pedestrians walking the sidewalks. People looked at them, but he went so fast, they hardly caught a glimpse of them before they were gone. He finally lost George after a few blocks but continued to run at full speed until they were safely at home. He wasn't even out of breath after running nearly six miles with his sister on his back.

"Wow," Melody said when Ezra placed her feet back on solid ground in their front yard.

"What happened back there?" She asked after a minute of silence.

"I saw the eyes! I saw them and I just panicked. After his weird questions and the things he knew about us, I just freaked out. We had to get out of there!" Ezra explained. He felt wired like he could run across town all over again, that was the adrenaline pumping through his body.

Melody completely agreed. She just hadn't expected her brother to run all the way across town at lightning speed with her on his back to get away from some creep. They were quickly interrupted by the slam of the screen door. Both of them looked up at the porch to see their mom coming outside with a surprised look on her face. She wasn't expecting to see them there. Ezra quickly came up with some story about Mr. Carson getting sick and dropping them off so they wouldn't have to wait for her to come to get them. She seemed confused but didn't ask questions before going back inside the house. This was the new Sarah. She didn't seem to ask as many questions like she just

30

didn't want to hear the answers. She was no longer the super involved, eager to hear every detail parent she once was. That felt so odd to Melody.

Sarah was standing at the kitchen counter preparing dinner when Melody came inside the house. She was quietly humming to herself. Sarah was pretty in an ordinary way. She had dark brown eyes instead of the brilliant hazel eyes flecked with gold Melody had. Her hair was kept cut in a long bob just at her shoulders. She had been getting it cut and colored the same auburn color since Melody could remember. She was thin and didn't look mushy and round like some of the other moms from school. Sarah was trendy but she also liked to be comfortable. This was apparent by her Tom's and flowy kimono. She took pride in her appearance even if all she did was look at books all day. Melody busied herself setting the table while she watched Sarah cooking.

Sarah, Cooper, Ezra, and Melody sat down at the table to have dinner together. With their mom's busy schedule running the store, they tried to have dinner a couple of times a week. Ezra thought this would be a great time to try to find out what their parents might know about these abilities. Maybe they could give away some clue about whether or not he and Melody were really aliens.

"Can I ask you something?" He didn't wait for an answer, "Do you know what those little gold boxes are for?"

Cooper choked on the water he had just swallowed. Sarah looked at him uncomfortably and took her time answering the question.

"I'm not really sure," she answered. "Hope that new music instructor is feeling better for your next lesson. I'd hate for you to miss another one so close to the concert," Sarah tried changing the subject and she looked to Cooper for some help guiding the conversation.

All of a sudden a weird noise came from the back of Melody's throat. She was groaning like she was in pain. Ezra looked at her and saw that she was bent over the table with her hands over both of her ears. She was sweating and her face was bright red.

"Honey, are you okay?" Sarah jumped up from her place at the table and went to Melody. She looked at Cooper and he got up from the table to come to Melody. Melody just groaned in response.

Ezra knew what was happening. She had explained the previous episodes to him in great detail. He wasn't sure what to do so he just sat there staring at his sister. The beautiful gold charm that hung around her neck was glowing. Ezra had never seen it do that before. He pulled the necklace out of his shirt and saw the tiny gold symbols

31

engraved in the charm were also glowing brightly. Melody suddenly grabbed her mother's wrist and looked at her. She realized that her mother had been acting so distant and hadn't been questioning the strange behavior and events because she knew something about what was happening to them but she wasn't telling them.

"You aren't telling the truth. Mom, what are the boxes and these necklaces and why is all of this stuff happening to us? You know, don't you?"

Chapter Four: A Prince and a Princess

Sarah pulled her arm away from Melody and took her seat back at the table. Cooper ran his rough hands over his face and through his dark hair. He looked at Sarah with fear in his eyes. Melody and Ezra watched them carefully waiting for someone to say something but they just stared at each other like they were waiting for the other to take the lead.

Before anyone could say anything, the house started to shake and the lights went out. Melody had a strong feeling of déjà vu when her father got up from the table to investigate, leaving them all in the dark. Melody wasn't sure what was going to happen next, but she did not want anyone else to leave the room. As the house started to shake harder and things fell from the walls, Melody heard the voices again in her head. This time, she could single out one loud voice that she thought she recognized. With all the noise, she didn't understand the words but she knew the voice. Melody screamed for her dad when she realized who the voice belonged to. Ezra got up from the table to check on their dad and she tried to stop him just like in her dream. Sarah looked both horrified and confused as Melody screamed for Ezra to come back over all the noise. She got up from the table and stumbled toward the junk drawer in the kitchen in search of a flashlight. Melody followed her every move with her eyes because she was scared to let another family member leave her sight. She got up and helped her mom light candles. She could still hear the sound of voices in her head over the noises of things crashing and falling throughout the house. None of this made sense to her. But Melody had this awful feeling in the pit of her stomach. This fear she was feeling was so ominous that Melody was afraid for their lives. She could tell that Sarah felt the same fear at that moment.

As Ezra walked cautiously through the shaking house, he kicked broken picture frames and called out for his dad. His eyes started to adjust to the dark when he saw a large shadow run past him in the hallway.

"Dad?"

Sarah and Melody joined Ezra in the hall with candles and a flashlight.

"I think Mr. Carson is in the house," Melody tried to tell Ezra but she wasn't sure if he would hear her over the sound of the house shaking and cracking.

The three of them walked together cautiously through the house calling out for Cooper. They never heard a response. When they entered the office, Ezra saw Cooper on the floor right away.

"Get her out of here," Ezra said to Sarah as he pushed Melody out of the room. Melody thought she saw blood on the floor near her dad's head before she was quickly escorted out of the room by her mother.

"No!" she screamed. "We aren't safe!"

"What do you mean, Melody?" Her mother looked her in the eyes.

"Mr. Carson is here. He hurt dad! I know he did!" Melody was hysterical. She was crying and fighting to get back in the office with her father and her brother. She wanted them to all be together and they would be safe. Melody knew something terrible happened in that room and wasn't going to stop until they let her in. Melody pounded on the door and kicked it.

When Sarah and Melody saw two figures pass by down the hall Sarah pulled them both back into the office. She wasn't sure how much Melody knew, but she needed to protect them now more than ever.

"Here, help me with this," Sarah shut and locked the door of the office and motioned for Ezra to help her as she pushed the large wooden desk in front of the door.

Melody just stood in the middle of the room staring at her father on the floor and she felt like all of the air had left the room. She wasn't sure if he was okay, but he didn't move or make a sound. She feared the worst.

As soon as the desk was in front of the door, something began banging on the other side. It sounded like something was trying to ram the door open as the wood started to crack. Sarah pulled Ezra and Melody close.

"I love you both as if you were my own," Sarah wiped the tears that had been silently streaming down Melody's cheeks and continued. "I should have told you everything before it was too late. Now there isn't any time. Take this and go to the bookstore," she said as she kissed them both on top of the head and shoved a small glass doorknob into Ezra's hands.

He looked at it, and then back at her. He wasn't sure what he was supposed to do with this.

"Here," she said, taking the doorknob back, "This will take you anywhere."

She touched an empty place on the wall with the knob as the banging on the other side of the door grew more frantic. She turned the knob and pulled. All of a sudden there was a door where there wasn't before.

"Go! Now!" she said pushing them both through the door. "I love you!"

As the door closed behind them, Melody heard the office door come crashing down and her mother scream. Ezra took the doorknob and put it in his pocket. Melody was crying and screaming for her parents. Ezra hugged her tighter than ever before. He looked around and saw that they were standing in the dark bookstore owned by their mother.

"Melody, look." He turned her toward the store. Moments ago they had been standing in their house with their parents while something banged the door down. Now they were smack dab in the middle of the science fiction section with shelves of books all around them. After everything that had happened in the last two weeks, this didn't seem as odd as it could have.

"What?" Melody was just as confused as Ezra as she scanned the surroundings.

She didn't want to leave the spot where they had entered the store. Melody wanted to go back for her parents. She wanted to make sure they were okay even though she knew deep down they weren't. Melody recalled the sound of splintering wood followed by her mother's screams. Something terrifying must have been on the other side of the door.

"Shouldn't we do something?" she asked.

"There isn't anything we can do for them now but keep going and find out what is happening. Don't you see that?"

"Ezra, it was Mr. Carson. I know it was. I heard him, like in my head," she placed her hands over her ears to demonstrate what she was talking about.

Someone broke into their home and hurt, possibly murdered their parents. They didn't know much else except that they couldn't go home, and their mom had sent them to the bookstore. So maybe there was something here that could help them. Ezra hoped that he could keep Melody safe here for the rest of the night.

Ezra and Melody decided to search through their mother's things in her back office. Sarah knew much more about what was going on than she had said. Ezra thought there might be something that could help them figure out what it was that she had kept from them. She had sent them to this place for a reason when she realized she had run out of time to tell them everything she knew. At home, Sarah was organized and neat. But her office was very different. She spent a lot of time tracking down rare books and doing historical research. She clearly didn't spend a lot of time organizing her office. It was cluttered with piles of papers on every surface. Melody switched on the desk lamp and started rifling through the papers on the desk while Ezra made his way to a set of filing cabinets on the side wall. By midnight they were both starting to get discouraged with what they found. Melody began crying again. She missed her parents and didn't know if she would ever see them again. She was tired and hungry. She didn't know where they were going to be safe. All of this was so overwhelming.

"We need to focus on trying to find out what mom was talking about. Mel. Can you hold it together and help me?" Ezra said sternly. He was clearly frustrated with his sister's crying and lack of help.

"Ezra! Why do you have to be so mean?" she yelled at him. She needed just a little time and space from him but was too scared to actually leave the same room as him so she turned her back to him and continued to cry while she dug through the papers scattered everywhere.

"Did you hear that?" Ezra quickly jumped to his feet leaving behind the pile of papers he had been sifting through hours earlier before he had fallen asleep.

He leaned toward the front of the bookstore to hear better. Melody sat up in the chair quickly and sat perfectly still straining to hear. Ezra thought he heard the sound of the front door unlocking and someone entering the store. As far as he knew, Uncle Simon was the only other person who had a key to the store. They both waited silently unsure of what to do next.

"Ezra, Melody," Simon said surprised to find them there.

Simon wasn't really their mother's brother but her best friend. He was like family to the kids so they always called him uncle. He was part owner of the bookstore with their mother. Melody let out the breath she had been holding as she had waited for someone to charge in after them. And Ezra sighed in relief. Both kids started crying as soon as they saw Uncle Simon enter the office. Simon pulled them to him with his large arms for a hug and tried to find out what was going on. But he couldn't understand a word they were saying.

"Take a breath. One at a time," he said.

Then Ezra and Melody told their uncle what had happened the night before in their home. Ezra was hesitant about how much they should tell him, but Melody was tired of the secrets. She felt that if she had told her parents the truth, maybe they wouldn't have gotten hurt. She didn't want to make the same mistake with Uncle Simon. He was all they had left. When they were finished, Uncle Simon sat silent for only a moment taking it all in.

"Follow me," he said as he left the office and went down the narrow stairs that led to the basement of the shop ducking so he wouldn't hit his head on the low ceiling.

The basement of the shop housed mostly storage. It was dark and dusty. Melody could smell mildew and watched for spiders as they followed behind Uncle Simon. He took his keys out of his pocket and unlocked a door that Ezra didn't even know was there. On the other side of the door was a small room with two bookshelves and two filing cabinets. Compared to the rest of the basement, this room was clean and tidy. It looked like someone cared for this room. Simon was silent for only a moment as the kids stared at him, confused.

"Kids, I have a lot to tell you. I'm not really sure where to start."

"I knew your birth parents. In fact, Sarah and Cooper knew them as well," Simon started.

"What do you mean you knew them?" Ezra asked.

"Many years ago, before you were born and even before I was born, my family came here like others before them. And by here I mean this world, this realm, or whatever you want to call it."

"What do you mean?" Melody asked. She was very confused, but he continued.

"Ezra, Melody, you also came from this other world. But I will get to that.

"Sarah and I always knew that we came from this other place. This other world is a world full of magic. It's a beautiful, amazing place.

But Sarah's great grandmother loved a man who wasn't from our world. He was without magical abilities. So she came here to start a family with him. Because of this Sara does not have any of this powerful magic her family once had, but instead, she gets to help protect its secrets. Here in these files and books is everything we know about the realm, about Athelage. We do simple things around here to keep Athelage and its magic secret. If people knew of the magic that really existed Athelage would be in danger. My family had a similar story. And that is how she became your guardian. From time to time, the kings and queens of Athelage would reach out to us for help with certain tasks, but usually, we just file away papers and explain magical occurrences away as science or fiction. One night ten years ago, they asked Sarah to take in these two sweet little children in order to keep them safe.

"I am afraid I don't know much about what she was protecting you from. Being outside of Athelage meant that there were limits to what they were able to share with us in order to keep us safe as well. But I am afraid it's no longer safe for you two here especially if we don't know what we are protecting you against."

Melody and Ezra looked at each other with puzzled expressions. They were full of questions and if it hadn't been for the strange things happening to them, they probably wouldn't have believed this story that Simon told them. However, they knew they were different already. Melody was starting to fear that Ezra was right in his alien theory, so she was a bit relieved to hear that they were just from some other beautiful, magical place. She wondered if it was the beautiful place that had been filling her dreams.

Ezra spoke first, "You said you knew our birth parents. Can you tell us about them?"

"Oh yes! I forgot! That is the most important part of the story after all! Your parents are the Royal Majesties King Ezra Ezeen Dragone VI and Queen Kasiah Adora Dragone," Simon bowed down to Ezra and Melody showing them the respect of a future king and queen.

Both children stared at him open-mouthed. Not only were they from another world, but they were royalty. This was all beginning to be too much for them to take in. Melody quickly sat down and looked to Ezra to say something.

"This is all a little much, Uncle Simon." Ezra shook his head trying to take it all in.

"I understand. I will give you guys a minute." Simon gave the kids a moment before continuing.

"What about the voices I've been hearing?"

"And my super strength?" Ezra asked.

"They must be part of your magic abilities. The magicians in Athelage all have different lines of abilities. Some are most powerful with fire or water. Some have more special tricks like mind control, telekinesis and so forth. And even more rare are masters of them all. The royal bloodline is strong with magic. But I was under the impression that your powers had been blocked as part of your protection. I am not sure what caused them to start working, but something must have broken the block or overpowered it. I am sure it is only the beginning of what you can really do."

It was finally starting to fall together for Ezra and Melody. Melody was so relieved to hear she wasn't losing her mind. Ezra couldn't wait to get more powers. All of this was exciting and fascinating, but the kids still just lost their parents. They still didn't know who was after them and where they would be safe. Melody was very overwhelmed, and Ezra felt guilty for this excited feeling he had over learning about his abilities and his birth parents when something bad might have happened to Sarah and Cooper.

"What kinds of powers do our parents have?" Melody asked.

"Queen Kasiah is a master of air and water. I have heard so many amazing stories about her use of the elements to help people all over the realm. King Ezra uses fire. He also has a very special mental ability of some kind. There aren't many details about it, but I have read that even as an infant he could manipulate objects with his mind." Simon laughed at the idea of a baby moving things with his mind.

"So what happened at our house?" Ezra asked worried about his parents.

"Someone must have found you. Years ago, the King and Queen believed that you were in danger. They were certain that they would be able to seek out and destroy this enemy by now. At which point, Sarah and Cooper were to give you a special gift that would allow you to return home. You would take your place as Prince and Princess and regain your powers. That's it! The gift," He said with a realization, "Did you receive a gift? That could have brought out your powers."

"Ezra, the necklaces!" Melody answered.

"Well, it seems that they were wrong, and your safety is still a concern. I think it might be for the best if we find a new safe place for you to hide until the time is right." Simon was nervous and sweating. He took his glasses off and rubbed them on his shirt.

Simon didn't look like the typical librarian like you might assume someone who owns a bookstore would. He was a tall, muscular man with short cut hair. He looked more like a bodybuilder than a well-read man, save for the glasses he wore. Being here with him made Melody feel safer than she did back at her house. But she didn't want to just find a place to hide. She wanted to find out what happened to her parents. She wanted to meet the King and Queen and see the beautiful place that Simon told them about. Melody wanted to find out more about herself and her birth family. She hoped Ezra felt the same way because she didn't think she would be able to do it on her own.

Before Melody could say what she was thinking, Ezra spoke up.

"No, Simon. It doesn't feel right to just go someplace and hide. We need to find out what happened back there. We have to help Sarah and Cooper especially after all they did for us all these years! And we need to go home! You can't just tell us about this beautiful place we come from and think we wouldn't want to go there."

Melody nodded. Simon was quiet for a moment, while he tried to decide.

"I guess you're right. Melody, is this what you want to do too?" Simon looked at her.

"Yes!" she said without hesitation.

"Well then, I guess it is settled. First, let's get you two something to eat and maybe a change of clothes. We should probably start looking through these files to see what we can find out about who came to your house last night."

Chapter Five: And Now Enter the Fighter

"Melody, come look at this!" Ezra sat with his legs crossed on the basement floor surrounded by files and books he had spent most of the afternoon looking at.

He held up a book for Melody to see. On the page was a picture of a beautiful couple. It looked like it was their wedding day. The woman was dressed all in white lace and sparkles. Her hair was a brilliant shade of blonde like warm honey. Her eyes were sparkling with happiness, and next to her was a man in an all black tux. He had dark brown hair slicked back and down past his chin. He was smiling at the woman in white with his arm around her small waist. They looked blissful and majestic.

"Is it them?" Melody asked.

Ezra knew who she meant and he nodded. They had been waiting practically all day to see a photo of their birth parents, and here it was, a picture of King Ezra and Queen Kasiah on their wedding day. They were so beautiful and happy that it made Melody cry. She took the book from her brother and sat down on the floor next to him so she could examine it closer. She was looking for some sort of resemblance in them. Looking closely at the picture, she could see they both had her mother's nose. Ezra had the same steely eyes as their father and they shared the same chin. Simon came over and looked over her shoulder at the picture.

"Ah! Such a happy day!" He said.

Both children waited for him to tell them more about this day, but he was silent at first as if enjoying the memory.

"This was a great day for Veya and for all of the people in Athelage. King Ezra was still just a prince. His father had been very ill and it was about time for Ezra to officially take the throne. He had gone away on a trip to learn about governance and to meet the people of his lands.

When he returned, he brought Kasiah with him. She was a beautiful, sharp-witted woman like none other. The people loved her instantly, and they thought she would be the best Queen they had ever seen. She was intelligent and knew so much about this realm. She had bright ideas for the future. Their wedding day came shortly after King Ezra's father, King Ezra V, passed away. The people had been in mourning and were happy to have a reason to celebrate. They were so glamorous and so much in love. It was rumored that they were already expecting you, Ezra, before the wedding."

Simon went on to describe a magical day filled with the most fragrant flowers in the land, the loudest music, and the happiest laughs. He gave so much detail, Ezra wondered if he had been there even though he told them he had never been allowed inside since his family had been outcast.

"King Ezra VI wedded to Queen Kasiah Adora on August 31, 2004, at the Grand Palace." Melody read the caption aloud.

Melody spent the next few hours studying the book Ezra had found. It contained more information about her father's reign and even her grandfather. While she learned all she could about their family, Ezra searched through other records and books to learn what he could about any enemies they might have. He didn't remember ever reading this much before in his life, but this was more important to him than school had ever been. Ezra read about places he never knew existed and beings he only heard of in fantasy stories. Could it be that these things really existed all along? If it wasn't for Simon, the kids would have read through breakfast, lunch, and dinner. But he was sure to make them stop and take regular breaks away from the stacks of books and papers.

Ezra filled in Melody on his discoveries during lunch. In between bites of his turkey sandwich, he explained some of the geography and history he had picked up from his reading.

"So, all of these places have been at peace for all these years. It's pretty crazy if you think about it. There hasn't been a war in a very long time and everyone just gets along from what I can tell. There are dwarves and elves and wizards. It's pretty cool. But it does seem like there is some kind of group, like a terrorist group out there trying to ruin everything. I'm not really sure what they have to gain," Ezra said.

"Ah, yes," Simon nodded in realization. It was like he was putting some pieces together.

"Each dominion possesses its own very powerful relic. They call them the Peacekeepers. These magical pieces were once a whole. A long time ago the different regions had been in turmoil untrusting each other for as long as they could remember. They all claimed to be the most powerful regions or the wealthiest or strongest and so on. Because of this a great wizard who was believed to be like a thousand years old made the Peacekeeper. Each region had an equal share of the power the world possessed from the magic relic making them all even and completely equal ending any argument and beginning the start of an alliance that has continued ever since," Simon recalled.

"But what does that have to do with this terrorist group?" Melody asked.

"Right. I have also heard that the group desires to destroy the relics with the belief that they could gain the power used in making them. This would make them more powerful than anyone else. They could do anything they wanted with that kind of magic, and no one would be able to stop them. It would be a very dangerous thing in the wrong hands, Melody."

"Aren't they worried about what that would do to Athelage?" Ezra didn't understand why they would risk so much.

"With that much power at stake, people get greedy."

It was while they were eating delivery pizza for dinner later that night that they started to develop a plan. They still knew so little about the potential enemy hunting them, but it was clear that King Ezra VI and Queen Kasiah had been taking steps to protect their people from something over the last decade. One of the books Ezra found outlined these strategies; walls built around the capitol, better training for palace guards and soldiers, money spent on ships and fortresses, and sending their two young children away from Athelage. Pictures showed construction and military training villages built for these purposes.

"I think we need a more updated inside source," Simon said after it seemed like they had searched through most of the materials he had stored away.

"What do you mean?" Ezra asked.

"I still have some connections inside Athelage. My cousin, Francesca brings me new information to file whenever a new textbook is printed. She likes to gossip and fill me in on the things going on. Not that I care about any of that, but she would be a good source for us.

She may be able to offer some assistance. It'd be wise to include her and I know we can trust her," Simon said.

If Simon trusted her then Ezra agreed.

"But how are you able to contact her?" Melody asked.

Simon explained how they sent messages between the realms using a cell phone. It was that easy. Francesca had a regular old cell phone. No magic there. Melody was slightly disappointed.

He quickly sent her a message asking her to meet him. She replied immediately.

"Well, that's settled. She should be here momentarily." Simon said this as if it was no big deal, but the kids couldn't believe it was that easy.

While they waited for Francesca to arrive, the children finished eating and picked up where they left off in their investigation. They had just gotten settled back in when there was a knock on the door upstairs. The kids raced up the rickety stairs behind Simon, anxious to meet Francesca of Athelage. But Simon stopped them.

"I don't want anyone to see you. Wait here." They waited in the stairway for Simon to come back with Francesca.

Francesca was roughly five foot tall and didn't look much older than Ezra. She wore her long black hair in a ponytail high on her head and a long black coat. Her pale eyes stood out against her tan complexion and her dark hair.

"Francesca, I want you to meet some friends." Simon put his arm out gesturing toward the two kids standing on the stairs. She looked as surprised to see them as they were her.

"They can't be," she whispered and covered her mouth. "Are they?" she looked at Simon in amazement.

Of course she knew right away who they were. They hadn't changed that much in all this time. She thought she was looking at two ghosts at first.

"Francesca say hello to Prince Ezra Ezeen VII and Princess Melody Estelle."

Francesca was surprised to see the prince and princess here. She explained to them that no one knew where they had been all of this time. Everything she knew was based on gossip around the villages. Some people believed that something terrible had happened to them. Others believed they were locked away in a tower hidden from the world. She was so honored to meet them and very curious.

"Francesca, this is a very delicate situation," Simon told her.

"What is that supposed to mean?" she put her hand on her hip and glared at her cousin.

"Keep your trap shut!" Simon sternly advised.

Clearly, he was concerned that the wrong person or people would find out they were there. He was doing his very best to keep the prince and princess safe, but he needed her help. She agreed to help them. After he filled her in on what happened at their home, she wanted to go to the house immediately and search for clues. Although Simon was tentative, she promised she would be able to keep them safe if the children came along.

"After all, I am a trained fighter now." She beamed.

Ezra and Melody looked at each other in surprise. How could this little thing be a fighter? And what exactly did that mean?

Simon agreed to let the children go back to the house, but he wanted to wait until morning. He didn't want to be in the house at dark if the power was still out. So they made a plan and Francesca was to return in the morning. As she made her way to the front door, Ezra asked how she was going to get home. The children were eager to learn as much as they could about the magic world they came from.

"I am not supposed to reveal our portal, but since you will one day be my king, I'll tell you. There are many secret passages between our worlds. Only a few of them are functioning anymore, but one of those passages is right down the street. It's in the warehouse by the river," she leaned forward and whispered to Ezra like it was a secret.

After Francesca left, Simon set the kids up to sleep. Melody slept on the leather couch in the small office, and Ezra made a bed on the floor beside her using the afghan Sarah loved. He wasn't planning on leaving her side if he could help it. Ezra also didn't plan on getting much sleep. His mind was racing from everything he learned, and he still had so many questions. He was anxious to go back to the house in the morning and to see Francesca again. While Melody slept peacefully, Ezra tossed and turned. No matter how hard he tried to sleep, he just couldn't. Being a teenager was hard enough without finding out that you are some magical being in hiding who will one day be a king of a realm you didn't even know existed.

By the time the sun began to rise, Ezra had only closed his eyes for what felt like a few minutes. Simon woke them up with donuts and juice. He wanted them to get some food in them before Francesca arrived to go check out the house. Simon wasn't a parent, but he

45

always took good care of them and looked out for them like a real uncle would.

"Ez, you look like crap. Did you get any sleep?" Melody asked as she rubbed the sleep from her eyes and attempted to comb through her hair with her fingers.

"Not really. But I'll be fine." He scarfed down a donut before Melody even took a bite.

Melody finished a donut and went to the bathroom next door to get cleaned up the best she could and ready to go back to their home. When she came out she saw Francesca sitting on the couch next to Simon waiting for her.

"Are we ready to go then?" Francesca smiled and asked.

"Do you have the doorknob?" Simon asked and Ezra dug it out of the pile of blankets on the floor.

"I am not really sure how it works," Ezra said holding the doorknob out.

"Place it anywhere on the wall with purpose. Know your destination, see it in your mind as you place it and turn the knob," Francesca explained as Ezra did just that.

When he pulled open the magic door that appeared like it had before, their living room was on the other side. Francesca went through the door first. Ezra stepped tentatively through before Melody and then Simon. They were all on high alert once they were through the door. The living room didn't feel like the same room anymore. This place did not feel like their home. It felt like a war zone after a bomb went off. All of their personal photos and papers were strewn around the room. A large table lamp that their mother had been excited to find at a thrift store was now lying on the floor with the cord ripped from the wall. It looked like a home after a tornado ripped it apart.

The house was silent when usually the sounds of their lives made the house feel warm and inviting. There weren't the sounds of music coming from Melody's room or video games from Ezra's. There was no typing from their mother's office or weights being lifted in the basement. Even the normal house noises, like the refrigerator, were missing.

The group stood in the living room cautiously looking around before proceeding through the rest of the house. They stayed close together unsure of what danger might be waiting for them. Francesca walked from room to room with the rest of them close behind carefully

46

looking in every corner. It was clear whoever did this was looking for something. All of the cabinets and drawers were emptied of their contents. The floor was scattered with papers and other personal belongings. But Ezra and Melody weren't sure if anything was taken from the house at first glance. The office was torn apart. The door was off the hinges and split in two pieces, but there was no sign of their parents.

"Whatever was here is gone now," Francesca said after they finished their walkthrough.

Ezra and Melody let out a sigh of relief in unison.

"Maybe they aren't dead," Melody said hopefully.

What would be the point of taking them if they were in fact dead? Since they weren't there, Melody was sure they were alive but taken somewhere. They were no closer to finding out who did this though, so Francesca wanted them to start searching the office for any clues. They didn't know what they were looking for, but Francesca assured them that they would know when they saw it.

They all stayed and searched the office together. Neither Francesca nor Simon wanted to let the kids out of their sight. Ezra and Melody went through the papers on the floor and put them back in the desk as they sorted them. Simon and Francesca picked up the pieces of the door and put them in the trash. They began to put the furniture back in order when Melody found something.

"Does this look familiar?" She handed Simon a small charm.

The charm was a small dragon and looked like it had fallen off of a chain. It was lightweight and silver. Simon looked it over carefully before he spoke.

"Yes, great job Melody. This looks like a dragon charm given to all of the Dragon Warriors of Veya." He handed it to Francesca to get her opinion.

"What's a Dragon Warrior?" Ezra asked excited that they were getting some answers. But Francesca was not happy when she spoke next.

"The Dragon Warriors are the King's personal guards."

"So you mean, the person responsible for all of this guards the King and Queen?" Melody asked afraid to hear the answer out loud.

"Yes! I am afraid we can't keep this to ourselves, Simon. I have to tell the King and Queen," Francesca replied.

It was obvious that now she was concerned for their safety. As an Athelage fighter, she was sworn to protect the kingdoms from threats, she explained. And this was certainly a threat. She thought that she should tell them personally if possible so that no one else would know. They didn't know who all was in on it and no one was to be trusted. No one.

Francesca escorted them safely to stay at Simon's house after the kids gathered some of their personal belongings to take with them. She was clearly nervous to leave the kids now that she knew what kind of danger they were really in, but she had to warn the King and Queen as quickly as possible. They took a portal using the doorknob to Simon's house that was on the other side of town. It was a large, brand new, four bedroom house on a man-made lake, too big for a single man. It was very clean and organized, unlike the normal bachelor pad. Simon seemed very particular about his things, but he told the kids to make themselves at home. They were too on edge to actually relax and do the things they would normally do. So after changing into their own clean clothes, the two kids sat together on the couch and continued reading through one of the history books they brought with them.

"This says that west of Veya there are mountains. The dwarves actually live inside the mountains. They like to be inside the caverns away from others and keep to themselves. And it snows like every day," Melody read to Ezra.

"I just saw something about the elves too. They live in a beautiful place where it's like spring every single day. It talks about beautiful lush woods and tons of wildlife that we probably wouldn't even know about. Do you think that means dragons and stuff are real too?" Ezra said.

"I guess it's possible, right? Anything seems possible now!" Melody replied thinking it over.

She carelessly twirled a strand of her hair around her finger like she usually did as she continued reading about the mountains of Warvelle and the short-tempered dwarves that lived there.

Hours passed before they heard from Francesca. Simon anxiously paced the house waiting for her to return. He kept looking out the windows and saying, "Where are you" under his breath. Melody wished she could will herself to read Simon's mind right about now. The more time passed, the more nervous they all were. Ezra was fixated on his parents and the guilt seemed to grow with every hour that went by without knowing what happened to them. It seems they had been doing even more for them than he even knew. They had risked their own lives by keeping him and Melody safe. Melody wondered if their parents had known the dangers of taking them in. Did they know that one day someone might come looking for them? Sarah and Cooper didn't deserve to be hurt, scared, or worse.

Ezra could tell that Melody was deep in thought. She was probably thinking about their parents too. He took her hand and mouthed, "It's okay." She nodded, but she didn't really believe him. This new world where they were a prince and princess with magical powers, and they were hiding out was frightening and dangerous. She was glad that she had Ezra though. At least he had super strength.

"Simon, how big is the Dragon guard?" Ezra asked as Melody and Ezra sat down in the spacious kitchen to keep him company.

"Over the years, the guard has grown. But there are only a handful of guards that are considered Dragon Warriors. These are the select few that the King trusts the most. They are the bravest, strongest of them all. According to my records, there are six Dragon Warriors."

Melody and Ezra sat in silence again. Simon was sure they had a lot of questions, but he was afraid to answer them out loud. He was glad they didn't ask. As the kids sat staring at the table, Simon began his pace around the house and checked each window again.

Melody was getting tired. She sat at the table with her chin rested on her arms trying to find the energy to stay awake. Just as she was feeling her mind relax and sleep creep in her ears started ringing. She heard a voice. As she tried to narrow in on the voice, Simon went to the front window. It was dark, and he had expected Francesca's return by now. And then he saw her, and Melody heard her. She was walking up the driveway at a quick pace. Simon and Melody met her at the door to let her in before she could be seen.

"I really should get myself one of those magical doorknobs," she said as she closed and locked the front door behind her.

Chapter Six: Finding the Monster

"Where have you been?"

"We thought you would be back by now?"

"How did it go?"

Simon, Ezra, and Melody all questioned Francesca at the same time.

"Whoa, give a girl a minute to catch her breath," she said, taking a seat on the couch.

They all hovered anxiously around her waiting for her to tell them what happened. Melody sat down on the couch next to her and mindlessly twirled her hair. Simon took up pacing the room again. Ezra just watched Francesca anxiously while she took a few deep breaths and tightened her ponytail.

Finally, Francesca was ready to talk. She had run all the way from the warehouse portal. Francesca said she was worried she might be followed and took precautions which led her way out of the way of the house before coming back.

"If anyone was following me from the warehouse, there is no way they stayed with me on that hike without me knowing. Anyway, things don't look very good guys. This is serious. I went to the palace and asked to speak with the King and Queen. The guards seriously looked at me like I was out of my mind for even making such a request, but I promised it was important and told them it was regarding the prince and princess. After a few minutes of talking with each other, they decided to let me in to see them. I was escorted by the guards to the throne room. I've never been in there when it was empty before. Usually during parties and things it is so crowded you can't tell just how big it is. Wow is it big!" Francesca spoke quickly. She continued to tell them about her wait in the throne room and King and Queen entering.

"Finally, King Ezra and Queen Kasiah entered the throne room. I asked if the guards could give us privacy as I had very important, secret information about the prince and princess. They didn't seem to want to be alone with me at first. I am sure they didn't think I'd have any connection to their children, and they were not sure if they could trust me. They are smart to keep their guards close to them everywhere they go. But eventually, the King asked the two guards posted at the door to give us a moment alone. "

Francesca told the King and Queen what had happened and how she was involved. She explained that it wasn't safe for Ezra and Melody and that their parents were missing. Lastly, she told them about the Dragon Warrior charm found at the house. King Ezra and Queen Kasiah were rightfully shocked and terrified. They expressed deep concern for Sarah and Cooper after all they had done for their children. They were torn on what to do. Queen Kasiah wanted to bring the children home immediately so that she would know they were safe, but King Ezra forbid it. He did not think they would be any safer in the palace if the person responsible was right under their noses. Who were they to trust now?

"Queen Kasiah, uh, your mother, said to tell you that she has missed you both deeply every single day. She said that she loves you both with every ounce of her being and cannot wait for the day that you can be reunited. She seemed very sad to talk about you being in danger again."

"So what are we supposed to do now?" Simon asked.

"They are going to investigate from within. King Ezra said there is one man he trusts to help him find the person responsible. There may be a few others that can help us, but for now, we are on our own. King Ezra has sent for all records of the guards coming and going at the portals. That is where we should start too. Maybe there are some cameras along the river that can help us see who uses that portal." Francesca said.

"That's a good idea, but how are we supposed to get access to cameras if there are any?" Ezra asked.

Francesca smiled and said, "You are too used to living in a world without magic, my dear Prince."

Ezra really felt funny being called prince. Ezra and Melody were curious to see what kind of magic Francesca could do and how it would get them the information they needed. But they sure were glad she was on their side.

"Francesca, do you know anything about how I can control my ability? It seems to come and go. I just can't get the hang of actually interpreting people's thoughts when it comes in like a jumbled mess, and I think it could help us" Melody said.

"Melody, we don't have time for that right now." Ezra didn't want Melody to impose on Francesca like that. He was sure there were other things they could be doing and he didn't want Melody annoying Francesca.

"It's fine. I think it is just going to take some practice. Maybe we should try." Francesca led Melody into one of the bedrooms and shut the door.

"We need quiet for this. Sit down and try to clear your mind. Have you ever meditated? It's kind of like that." She said quickly, excited to be able to help Melody.

"No, not really. But I am willing to try." Melody closed her eyes and did what Francesca said.

Melody sat straight and followed Francesca's instructions to try to relax every part of her from her toes to the hair on her head. They sat there in silence for several minutes as Melody focused on her breathing. As she did this, she began hearing the ringing in her ears and then there was the sound of a muffled voice like someone under water. She concentrated and tried to keep herself relaxed. Then Melody heard Francesca's voice inside her head.

"This would be a great tool in finding out the enemy if we can get her to control it." Francesca thought.

Melody gasped and jumped up!

"I heard that! And you are right! If we can get in front of the Dragon Warriors and I can read their thoughts, we can find out who is responsible!"

Francesca wondered how close Melody had to be to someone in order to clearly read their minds. So they put it to the test. They spent the next hour with Francesca moving around the house while Melody tried to read her thoughts. After another hour of practice, Melody was able to read her thoughts clearly with a little less effort even though it was more challenging the farther away she was. She wasn't able to hear Francesca's thoughts when she went outside of the house, but she somehow still felt she was near. Melody was starting to even feel Francesca's presence and be able to tell where she was when she could not see her. She tried to explain it to Ezra as she sat by him and tried to become more familiar with how his thoughts felt when he was close, but it was just a feeling she had she couldn't really explain to him.

"I think that's enough for tonight," Simon said. He settled the kids into bedrooms of their own while he and Francesca retreated to the kitchen to discuss their next moves.

Simon was adamant about not letting the kids out in public. They weren't sure who they should be looking for, and it was too dangerous for them. After arguing for an hour, Francesca was able to convince Simon that she needed their help, but only Ezra would be allowed to go with her the next day to scope out the area near the portal for cameras. He had super strength that could come in handy if anything bad happened. Simon would keep Melody at the bookstore, and she wasn't going to be happy about it. He told Francesca that he would find things to keep her busy while they were away so she didn't feel too left out. He knew Melody was eager to learn about her birth family and Athelage. Any twelve-year-old girl would be excited about finding out she was a princess, and Melody wasn't any different. He would show her more pictures of the beautiful kingdom of Veya and events at the palace over the years. That was sure to impress her.

Everyone slept a little easier with Francesca under the same roof that night. She was small, but she was a trained fighter sworn to protect Veya. This sounded like an important title the way she said it, and she had proved she was useful so far. Melody and Ezra had not seen what she was capable of yet, but knowing that Simon trusted her to keep them safe was enough for them.

Ezra felt well rested when morning came. He almost couldn't believe it was morning already as he opened his eyes and looked around the strange room he had spent the night in. The room was bare except for the full-size bed and single dresser in the corner. It occurred to Ezra to ask Simon why he might need so many extra bedrooms. He might ask him if he remembered.

As Ezra was digging through the gym bag of belongings he brought with him, he pulled out the golden box that had once held the magic trinket he now wore on a chain around his neck. This little present was meant to bring them home one day and restore their powers. He said a quick little prayer under his breath for Sarah and Cooper hoping they were alright. Ezra got dressed and found Francesca and Simon in the kitchen.

"You are coming with me, kid," Francesca said with a grin. Francesca seemed very tough on the outside, but she was also playful. Ezra liked that about her.

"Great! Where are we going, exactly?"

"We are going to go check out the area near the portal downtown. Get ready."

Ezra was excited to get out of the house and do some more investigating. He thought he might get a chance to find out what other magic existed and what Francesca could do with her powers. And the longer they went without finding anything about Sarah and Cooper the more worried he became. More than anything else, he wanted them to be safe and he wanted to be useful. He could live without the magic again if he had to, and he would even go back to hiding if it meant Sarah and Cooper were safe.

Ezra didn't even know if Francesca was old enough to drive, but she was behind the wheel of Simon's Buick driving them toward the empty warehouse by the river. Somehow it just felt strange looking at a mysterious, magical being behind the wheel of an ordinary luxury sedan. She seemed to know what she was doing as she maneuvered the car through town in silence. As they pulled up in front of the warehouse, they both started looking for signs of anyone else being there today. Francesca got out of the car, and Ezra followed her. They began walking around the building in search of any surveillance cameras on any of the surrounding buildings and street posts. They were about to give up when Francesca spotted it.

"Look!" She was thrilled to find something useful. High above them in a fourth story apartment window was a camera. It wasn't easy to see, but it looked like it was pointed directly at the street and the front door of the warehouse would be directly in its view.

"Great, but now what?" Ezra didn't share Francesca's enthusiasm over spotting the camera. He had no idea how she thought she was going to get to that camera.

"Just follow my lead." Francesca raced across the street to the crumbling brick building that had long ago been turned into apartments.

Ezra hesitated a moment before following her inside the building and up the stairs to the fourth floor. The building smelled funky, like a mixture of sweat, spicy food, and stale cigarette smoke. The walls were yellowed and peeling. Years of dirt and grime went neglected on the stairs. Ezra caught up with Francesca who was standing in front of a door marked 4B just as she was about to knock. Ezra had butterflies in his stomach when the occupant of apartment 4B opened the door. He wasn't sure what Francesca was going to say to this scruffy looking man to get him to show her the camera.

"Good morning sir. I'm Detective Santiago with the PPD. We are investigating a string of crimes in this area. We noticed you have a camera there." Francesca flashed a piece of paper like a badge to the confused man standing in the doorway.

"Uh yeah. I got that camera there a while back when someone kept messing with my car." The guy was thin with messy hair and an unshaven face. By the looks of his apartment, he didn't have much that was nice but the camera looked pretty high tech.

"Do you mind if we check it out?" Francesca entered the man's apartment as he walked over to where the camera was in the window.

"Sure, no problem." He handed her the camera.

Ezra didn't know how this guy actually believed that they were detectives. They were two kids. But here they were, standing in his apartment looking at the camera. Francesca took the memory card from the camera and told the man that she would be taking it with her.

"How in the world did that work?" Ezra asked when they got back outside. Adrenaline was rushing through him at this point. He couldn't believe that had worked and they were now in possession of the memory card from the camera.

"Magic," Francesca laughed and walked back to the car.

On the way back to Simon's with the memory card, Francesca told Ezra that she had a special ability that allowed her to convince people of anything. It usually only worked on people who did not possess power, because other magicians could sense when her power was creeping into their mind.

"What else can you do?" Ezra asked.

Francesca showed him a set of charms she wore around her ankle. There were several charms hanging from the anklet, each representing its own unique power that Francesca possessed.

"Wow! How do you have so many?" Ezra asked.

"Some of them I learned. Like this one here," she pointed to trinket with a symbol that looked like a wave. "It allows me to control water. I had to study and work hard to earn it. These kinds of powers are dangerous and you really have to know what you are doing to manipulate the elements. And some I was born with like you. When I get a little older, I will have all of these symbols as tattoos to represent my strength. It is customary for fighters to in Veya to have tattoos to represent their skills and abilities."

"That's so cool!"

Francesca drove the car quickly to the bookstore so they could look at the video footage. Simon had taken Melody there to continue searching through the records in the basement to keep her busy. When they got there, Melody was not happy about being excluded from the trip.

"Simon, get your computer. We found some video footage we need to look at," Francesca rushed.

Anxious to see what the camera might have caught, they all gathered around the laptop while Simon pulled up what was saved on the card. The excitement faded after a while as they all watched the footage of the street between the apartment and the warehouse with nothing happening. They sped through hours and hours of cars driving by and people walking on the sidewalk without seeing anyone coming or going from the warehouse beside Francesca.

"I'll keep looking at this. I think you should see if you can find out about the substitute singing instructor that Melody mentioned. That might be our best lead now," Simon said to Francesca. "Ezra will go with you."

Melody crossed her arms across her chest and slumped her shoulders. She was not happy to be left out of another field trip.

Ezra gave Francesca directions to the music academy where Melody took singing lessons. As they drove down the streets, it was hard for Ezra to see things as they had always been. So much had changed in his life the last few days that he couldn't imagine everyone else still going about their lives as if it was the same. But everyone was still carrying on with their normal lives as if magic didn't exist. His friends were still going to school and sitting in boring classes. There were baseball practices he was missing. Cooper wasn't at his job like he should have been. He wondered how long it would be before people started to notice they were all missing.

They went straight to the office on the first floor to speak to the secretary. Once again, Francesca pretended to be a detective. She was very vague about why she was there, but the administrator and office staff seemed to believe her without question. They told her that Ms. Capechio had left suddenly on a family emergency and another instructor had stepped in. They didn't seem to know much about him and still had not heard from Ms. Capechio about when she would return. It seemed highly suspicious to Francesca and Ezra, but the administrator seemed to have bought it. It took some convincing, but Francesca and Ezra were able to get a mailing address for George Carson, the substitute instructor.

"I don't think Simon would be happy with us if we went and checked it out," Ezra said as Francesca entered the address into the car's GPS.

"That is why we aren't asking for his permission." Francesca pulled the car out of the parking space and headed toward the destination she had input.

They pulled up to the house guided by the GPS voice. It was a pretty average looking house from the outside. It was a small one story box house that looked almost identical to its neighbors. The flowers in the front yard were dead or dying, and the grass needed to be cut. Nothing really seemed out of the ordinary except that the mailbox was full. Francesca got out of the car first, and Ezra hesitated a moment before he followed. He wasn't ready to be face to face with Mr. Carson again.

Francesca was busy peeking into the front windows when Ezra joined her on the front porch of the plain white house.

"Doesn't look like anyone's home," She walked around the back and tried the doorknob. It was locked. "We will just have to let ourselves in then," Francesca smiled mischievously at Ezra.

She seemed so comfortable with the fact that they were about to break into the house of the man who quite possibly was after them and had kidnapped his parents. Ezra was trying so hard to be brave and not appear weak in front of her, but this was terrifying. He wiped the sweat from his palms on his jeans, took a deep breath and then broke in the door easily with his shoulder.

"Thanks, muscles!" Francesca said and stepped into the house first.

Francesca directed Ezra to be the lookout while she checked the house. Quickly, she went about searching the house for clues about Mr. Carson. However, his house lacked any kind of personal effects. In fact, it was hard to believe that anyone actually lived here. The house was spotless, there was no food in the cabinets or refrigerator, the bed was made and the closet was empty. The only thing Francesca found was a stack of mail on the table.

"This guy is definitely suspicious," Francesca stated the obvious.

As they were about to call off the search and head back to the bookstore, Ezra spotted a car pulling into the driveway. Francesca yanked him into a hall closet and clasped her hand over his mouth.

They listened quietly as someone entered the house. Ezra felt the adrenaline racing through him as he started to shake. The person on the other side of this door was the same person who hurt his parents, he just knew it. He wanted so badly to be able to do something about it, but at the same time, he did not want to jeopardize the investigation or get Francesca hurt. So instead he waited silently with Francesca and listened through the door.

They heard the man's voice. It sounded like he was talking to someone.

"I got them through the portal to the safe house. Don't worry about that. No one saw me." He was definitely talking to someone on the phone.

"Those brats were clueless when they saw me. They could have taken me out then but didn't. I am sure they had no idea what they were capable of. It couldn't have gone any better than it did with them running like that, and the McCarthys are locked away tight," he paused as if he was waiting for the person on the other line to finish speaking before he continued. "I know what I'm doing boss."

The call ended and they heard the man close the bathroom door. Francesca used her hands to gesture like she was turning a doorknob and Ezra realized she was asking him for the magic doorknob. He pulled it out of his pocket and handed it to her. Francesca used it quickly to take them back to the bookstore with Simon and Melody.

Melody practically jumped out of her skin when Francesca and Ezra appeared out of the wall.

"Try knocking next time!" she shouted and Ezra couldn't help but laugh.

Ezra stuck the doorknob back in his pocket, thankful that he had it with him when they left.

"Did you find anything?" Simon asked Francesca as he entered the office.

"You aren't going to be happy, but we went to George Carson's house. The place looked like no one lived there, but he does. He showed up, and we overheard him on the phone. He definitely took their parents, but I couldn't figure out who he was talking to. He knows they have abilities, but I don't know how much he knows. That George Carson is most certainly a changeling. I could smell it on him," Francesca cringed at the thought of the smell.

Needless to say, Simon was furious, and rightfully so if George Carson was what Francesca thought. But he was also glad to hear the information. Turns out, he and Melody had also seen George Carson. They had been watching the video footage and saw him enter and leave the warehouse several times over the last couple of weeks. And he wasn't always alone. In one of the shots from the video camera, Melody saw the creepy substitute teacher walking through the warehouse door with a woman that could have been her real music teacher.

"I think I should check in with the King and Queen. See if they found anything else out and let them know what we have," Francesca said.

"We want to go with you this time," Ezra said. Melody nodded in agreement. She was ready to go to Athelage and meet the King and Queen.

"I don't think so," Simon said adamantly against the idea. Francesca agreed with him, but she looked like she was considering it.

"It's only a matter of time before they find us just hiding out here. If we go, we might be of more use there. Someone there is helping him, and we need to find out who. We aren't going to get anything else from these tapes. So what is the next move?" Ezra asked.

"He may be right," Francesca said to Simon.

"If that is what you want to do, I can't really stop you. Just know that I think you will be putting yourselves at risk by going. You will be somewhere completely foreign and possibly even more dangerous. There is no way to know what we will be going into," Simon said.

"Alright, let's go!" Ezra said.

Chapter Seven: Athelage Here We Come

Considering how quickly Francesca recognized the long lost Prince and Princess of Veya, Melody and Ezra donned their best disguises in preparation for Athelage. Melody wore a jet black wig and a large hat to cover her face. Ezra put on a giant sweatshirt with the hood up. Francesca insisted they would have to wear the disguises to make it safely to the palace without drawing any unwanted attention. If necessary she could use her power of persuasion, but that had to be the last resort. Melody got the feeling that Francesca's power of persuasion wasn't a sure thing when it came to using it on her own kind. But she had to admit, she was jealous Ezra got to see her use the power.

Melody had a pit in her stomach the size of a watermelon as they readied to leave and used the magical doorknob to take them to the warehouse that housed the magic portal. This was such a monumental moment for her and Ezra. They would finally get to meet their birth parents after all this time of wondering about them. Not only that, but they were a king and queen of a magical world that Ezra and Melody would have to use magic to travel to in order to be reunited.

"Is this my life," Melody heard her brother's thoughts momentarily and she nodded.

Ezra tried to prepare himself mentally for the moment when they met the King and Queen, but he really didn't know what to expect once they went through the portal. His hands were shaking as he stepped through the door he created in Simon's paneled dining room wall. He prayed that they were able to make it safely to the palace without being spotted. He hoped his parents were as happy to see him as he was.

More than anything, he prayed that he could keep his sister safe from the unknown.

"Ready?" Francesca asked as they stood in front of a door marked "janitor" inside the abandoned warehouse. The portal must be on the other side of this door.

The kids looked at each other. Ezra grabbed Melody's hand and nodded. The future King and Queen of Athelage took a step through the doorway and a giant leap into their future. Ezra and Melody saw the blue hazy circle suspended in midair right inside the doorway. It looked just like Ezra had imagined it would.

"Let's not waste time," Melody said hoping she sounded more confident than she felt as she squeezed her brother's hand a little tighter and stepped toward the portal.

Francesca led the way as the four of them went through the spinning portal that would lead them to Athelage. Melody felt weightless with her first step and the next thing she knew she was blinded by the bright sun in a whole new world. This was the place she would one day rule.

Melody squinted as her eyes took time to adjust. She could hear the sounds of birds and insects. She could smell a mixture of fresh dirt, grass, and sweet flowers. When she could finally see what was around her, she stood there for a moment taking it all in. They were in a meadow surrounded by tall grass. In the distance, she could see mountains and hear water trickling from a spring. The hills to the north were spotted with purple and red trees just like Melody had dreamed. There didn't appear to be any civilization nearby. It was nearly dusk back home, but here the sun was high in the sky like it was only noon. It was all so familiar to her from the dream she had been having over the last several months. The sense of familiarity allowed her to put her guard down. This was her home.

"Where do we go now?" Ezra asked, clearly confused.

Francesca pointed toward the mountains.

"The capital and the palace are just on the other side of those hills. My power isn't quite strong enough to transport us all there. So we will have to walk. It will take us a few hours to walk there so we better get started."

Ezra, unable to use his super speed because the others wouldn't be able to keep up, tried to keep a slow steady pace. As they walked Francesca told them about the capital city and what to expect while Simon filled in details where he could. She explained that this was one of the only ways into the city in order to protect it. The guards would be alerted the second they stepped through the portal and would have plenty of time to prepare for any kind of attack, but they would probably ignore a small group like them. In the years before the kids were born, there had been many other portals and ways into the city were endless, Simon explained. But this was before when the king and queen were safe and the world was at peace. There was no need to monitor the people coming and going.

Melody followed along quietly as she continued to survey the surroundings. Everything in the meadow was beautiful. The colors and smells were more vibrant and the sounds more musical. Just being in Athelage made Melody feel less anxious than she had been moments before. Ezra still seemed to be on edge, however. His jaw was clenched tight and his hands were balled into fists at his side. Ezra was ready for an attack just in case he needed to protect his sister. As they continued walking, Melody started to struggle to keep up.

"Do you need a break?" Francesca asked.

"Surely there is an easier way to get there," Melody sat down in the grass where they stood and rubbed her feet.

"Mellie, I can carry you the rest of the way," Ezra offered.

He knew he could run for long distances without tiring and didn't think that he would have a problem carrying his sister on his back for the rest of the walk. She didn't look pleased to go riding in on her brother's back. She didn't want to look like she was weak in front of Francesca and Simon who clearly weren't having any problems with the walk. But she agreed so they could get there faster. She knew she was holding them up.

"When we get there, we must walk quickly to the palace without stopping. There will be a lot you will want to look at, but you must remember to keep walking and looking down. We can't have you recognized. The news would spread so fast that whoever is after you would probably know we were there before we even get to the King and Queen. Remember, we don't know who we can trust," Francesca insisted with her stone cold look of seriousness.

"Are there other kingdoms nearby?" Ezra asked.

He was surprised by the vastness they were welcomed by arriving through the portal. He read about the mountains where the dwarves lived and the forests filled with elves, but he didn't see any of that here.

"There are other kingdoms and villages in Athelage filled with magicians. Some are much smaller, but your parents rule the largest kingdom of Athelage named Veya. Their rein also includes many smaller towns to the west. The mountains are far in that direction too," Simon answered as he pointed toward the left.

They hiked up the side of the cliff following a path that had been worn into the side of the mountain from years of feet treading back and forth from the kingdom. The sun was high in the sky when they made it to the top of the mountain. Melody still couldn't believe how bright the sun was but despite the sun beating down on them, the temperature was perfect. The combination of the heat, the smell, and the sounds reminded Melody of the perfect spring day. She wondered if it was always this beautiful as she saw a bright pink butterfly land on a nearby flower like she had never seen before. The deep purple and green of the flower were vibrant and bold.

Ezra stopped at the top for a moment as he took in the view from the top. The kingdom was just below them. It felt so close now, and he couldn't believe they were actually seeing it. He could see pops of bright colors down in the city behind an ancient stone wall. Smoke came from the chimneys of houses and shops. As he looked closer, it appeared the pops of color were the people walking the paved streets of the town. Melody gasped when she saw the palace right in the center of the town. The place where her parents lived towered above all the other buildings. It was the tallest thing she had ever seen. She had pictured a large, ancient stone palace from an ancient civilization, and she was not disappointed. It was much larger and grander than she had anticipated with large rounded windows, gray stone that was worn from age, and she thought she could see a drawbridge even. It was hard to tell from so far up, but it looked like it was 20 stories tall. Seeing the moat around the palace, Ezra wondered how it would protect them if the danger was already inside.

"Let's keep going," Francesca lead the way down the narrow path toward the town. Ezra picked up the pace anxious to finally reach their destination. When they were right outside the stone walls, Ezra placed Melody back on the ground. She straightened her wig and took a deep breath. Her heart was racing, and her palms were sweaty as she walked through the large doors in the wall and entered the kingdom. Simon looked as anxious as Melody felt. Melody hadn't thought about what a big moment this must be for him too. She imagined he had spent his whole life learning about Athelage but had never actually seen it with his own eyes until now.

The town was full of activity. The paved streets were large enough for cars and included paths for the people to walk on. The shops and houses that lined the streets were all made of stone. Ezra was reminded of a science fiction movie about time travel when he saw all the worn wood, stone, and straw building materials. But all of the fixtures and decorations Ezra could see looked bright, shiny, and new. Some people walked quickly down the streets like they were in a hurry to complete their tasks. Others took their time mulling about stopping to chat. Melody could feel the presence of magic all around them. It was like an energy that soaked into her bones and made her vibrate from the inside. The people that walked the streets all wore bright beautiful robes. Many of the people had bright colored hair and makeup to match. She also noticed necklaces and chains filled with trinkets similar to her own charm. People were using magic openly on the streets. Magic spells were used to make their bags float beside them freeing their hands. They used magic to open doors and wash store windows. It was everywhere around them. Melody tried to keep looking forward and not to act out of place as they followed Francesca toward the center of town. Francesca walked with purpose and stood out in her all black clothes. Melody wasn't sure if that was a fashion choice or more of a uniform for her position. Others didn't seem to pay any special attention to her in black. She motioned for them to keep up the pace as she made her way through the crowds.

Ezra feared that someone would stop them. Someone walking alongside them might recognize them and start shouting. He thought it was possible the person responsible for the attack, might be right here watching them. They might not even make it to the palace to see the King and Queen. In his mind, he saw everything going wrong. This all had just been too easy. But no one stopped them. No one even seemed to notice them as they walked quickly and quietly through the town toward the palace. They were almost to the King and Queen. He wondered what it would be like. What they would be like.

They crossed over the moat on an ancient drawbridge and made their way to the door. There was a single guard standing at the door. He seemed to recognize Francesca from her recent visit as he did not ask any questions before he opened the heavy doors for them to enter. Now that they were closer, Melody gazed at the palace in disbelief. She could tell now that it was maybe only five or six stories tall, but it still felt giant as they entered the main foyer of the mansion. Everything was sparkling white and gilded with gold from the floor to the silky drapes that hung from the large windows in the room. There was a large marble staircase in the center of the room and a bright crystal chandelier. Ezra noticed banners that lined the balcony overlooking the foyer. Each banner was made of a bright colored cloth with a different gold symbol in the middle. The symbols looked ancient and beautiful.

Francesca led the group past the staircase toward the center of the first floor. The kids tried to keep up with her as she walked with purpose toward the throne room and they removed their disguises. Simon was taking it all in with fresh eyes alongside the prince and princess. He was making mental notes to file away for later, Ezra was sure. Francesca didn't hesitate when she got to a set of large, heavy doors and pushed them open. Ezra gave Melody's hand a quick squeeze with his sweaty palm to reassure her before they followed Francesca into the room.

With her heart racing, Melody didn't have much time to prepare for what was about to happen. She was about to enter this room and meet her birth parents, the parents that gave her away to save her life. She was going to be in the same room as royalty from another dimension she just learned existed. It all seemed like too much at once, but when Ezra squeezed her hand, she felt a little more confident. She remembered that she wasn't going through this alone, and no matter what happened she still had her brother. He must be scared too, but he was doing his best to make her feel at ease. She appreciated that about him. They didn't always get along, but he always looked out for her when it really mattered.

The throne room was enormous just like Francesca had described it. It was a circular room that appeared to be the heart of the palace. The floor was made of white marble with thin gray veins. There were large marble columns around the edges of the room that seemed to be holding up a sort of viewing gallery above. The walls were covered in shiny gold that could have been wallpaper or actual gold. And at the center of the room hung the most magnificent chandelier anyone had ever seen. It was bright and shiny. It must have had over thousand lights. Melody took it all in before she saw what she was really looking for. At the far end of the room opposite the door raised on a slight platform were two gold thrones with carved dragons on the top. And sitting in those thrones were Queen Kasiah and King Ezra.

Francesca approached the thrones first. She bowed deeply to show her respect and Simon nervously followed her lead. Melody and Ezra hesitated and then followed behind Francesca. As they got closer, Melody could see herself and Ezra in their birth parents. She had seen it before in the pictures, but being here, right in front of them it was undeniable. Her mother's long dark blonde hair shined under the chandelier. She had the same round face and eyes as her mother. She saw Ezra's jawline in their father. Ezra bowed low and Melody copied him.

With his head bowed, Ezra heard a small laugh.

"Get up," the King said in a smooth even tone. He seemed humored by them bowing.

When Ezra lifted his head, he saw a smile on the King's face. Queen Kasiah smiled back at King Ezra as they looked at each other. And then she stood up from her throne. She smoothed her deep purple gown with her hands and stepped down from the platform toward them and the smile on her face grew larger as she looked at each child.

"Ezra," she said softly as she touched his cheek and turned to Melody.

She grabbed Melody's hand and tears began to fall from her hazel eyes silently. Before the children realized it, King Ezra was behind her pulling them all into a hug with tears of joy streaming down his cheeks as well. The hug seemed to go on forever but not long enough all at the same time. Melody cried into her mother's shoulder and hugged her father back. She had always wondered what her birth parents would be like, but she had never thought she would actually get the chance to meet them. She always thought that it was possible they didn't want her, but standing in this hug she knew that was not the case. She could feel the love they had for her and Ezra. She could feel just how heartbreaking it had been to have to give them away. She could feel the joy of their return after all this time. Melody felt the fear of being under attack and she felt the sadness from the loss of Sarah and Cooper. All of these feelings flooded over them all through that one big hug.

King Ezra pulled away and took a moment to wipe the tears from his face before he spoke.

"I can't believe you are here."

The joy from their reunion was replaced with a look of fear.

"Why did you bring them here? You know it isn't safe," King Ezra spoke to Francesca.

"Your Majesty, I understand. But I couldn't keep them away any longer. We did bring some news," Francesca explained.

66

The King nodded and waited for Francesca to continue, but Ezra spoke this time.

"We saw the man we thought was George Carson, a music teacher, coming and going through the same portal that Francesca has been using for some time, and on one of his trips through the portal it looked like he had the real music teacher with him. It is possible that he kidnapped her to take her place in the school. We also heard him talking on the phone with someone about our parents, uh the McCarthy's. It seems he is working with someone else, but we aren't sure who. We were hoping maybe you had found something."

Queen Kasiah explained that they were suspicious of anyone on the palace guard. They had put the palace on complete lockdown and their most trusted guard had been secretly investigating. He had found some incriminating evidence against a few guards but nothing that linked them to the attack yet.

"Maybe we can find a way to link this George Carson to one of them. We have three guards locked up that we should question immediately."

With that, King Ezra left the room to speak with his personal guard quickly. He returned just as quickly to his children.

"How about a tour of the palace?" King Ezra sounded excited to show the children around as he clapped his hands together and headed out of the throne room once more.

King Ezra was a big man with a big personality. He made large gestures with his hands while he spoke and guided them around. King Ezra told stories of the short time they lived in the palace all together and of the things that had been changed since they had been gone. He smiled from ear to ear and his eyes sparkled as they walked around the palace. Although the circumstances were less than pleasant, he had waited for this moment for so long. He smiled from ear to ear at the fact that he was united with his children once again. Clearly, his family was very important to him. All of the years stressing about where his children were and hoping that he could keep them safe had taken a toll on him. His hair was graying and his frown lines were very prominent on his face. Ezra imagined that he had not had much cause for celebration over the last ten years.

Each room of the palace was filled with treasures of this world. Melody noticed foreign symbols and markings on antiques and beautiful paintings everywhere she looked. The rooms seemed to grow larger than the one before it as they made their way toward the private chambers of the King and Queen. There were even rooms set up for Ezra and Melody.

"We knew that one day our children would be able to return to us. It's important to us that you know this is your home even after all this time," Queen Kasiah explained the bedrooms they had set for them.

Ezra's room was fit for a king with oversized, mahogany furniture that looked handcrafted with fine details. Each piece had tiny little designs engraved in gold. A portrait of baby Ezra with his mother and father hung from the deep blue wall. Ezra stared at the painting of the King and Queen gazing at an infant wrapped in a white blanket. He saw how happy the King and Queen were staring at their perfect little baby. The portrait was filled with so much love. He thought about how hard it must have been for them to send this little boy away and miss out on so much over the years. The fear that led them to send their babies away was still very real. Whatever caused this fear was still out there.

The four-poster bed and matching furniture in the princess' room was all white. And the bed was covered in plush purple pillows; such a royal color. Melody's bedroom had a similar portrait hanging on the wall. A young Queen Kasiah held an infant daughter dressed in white. King Ezra held a toddler with curly blonde hair next to them. The family of four in the painting looked so happy. It made Melody wonder what her life would have been like here, growing up in this room. How would her life have been different? What about Sarah and Cooper?

It was hard to enjoy their first time in the palace since they were babies when everyone was on edge. The King escorted the four of them to a sort of living room area after the tour, leaving them with Simon and Francesca for a short time so that he could assist in questioning the guards. Queen Kasiah left to meet with a council. Melody thought she seemed nervous as she said her goodbyes.

"Why do you think she's so nervous?" Melody asked Francesca after the King and Queen had left.

"I am sure she doesn't know who she can trust even in her own council. I wonder if they even know where you have been this whole time," Francesca explained as she examined the artwork hanging on the wall.

"I wish I could help them. Maybe I should have gone with the King. I could tell which guards were telling the truth. Or I could have helped the Queen know who she could trust in the council." Melody said.

"I don't think it's worth the risk to them," Ezra replied.

He sure didn't want to risk his sister by having her try out her new power on potentially dangerous magicians from another world. Melody felt the time pass slowly as she waited for the King and Queen to return. They were all anxious to find out the outcomes and jumped at every sound outside the room not feeling entirely safe here in the palace. Ezra paced the large room. He pretended to be interested in checking out the artwork that hung on the walls and the figurines that covered a bookshelf along one wall, but he couldn't really focus his attention on any of it.

Out of boredom, Melody thought she would try out her new power. She sat in a fluffy chair in the corner of the room away from the others and concentrated on relaxing every part of her mind as she had practiced with Francesca. She imagined her mind reaching outside of the room to feel if anyone else was around. At first, she didn't feel or hear anything.

She let out a sigh of frustration and tried to refocus her energy. Melody tried again. She slowed her breath and relaxed her mind and body. Again she imagined her mind reaching outside of the room and down the halls of the large palace. She felt herself moving throughout the white rooms although her body was still seated in the living room with her brother, Simon, and Francesca. And then she felt it.

First, it was just the feeling of a presence. Melody wouldn't have been able to explain it to someone if they had asked what it was like. But she knew that someone was there. It could have been a guard or a member of the palace staff. It could have been pretty much anyone. She didn't hear anything though, not at first. But she pushed harder. Just as Melody was about to give up she heard it!

"How did they get past Carson? What are they doing here?" the thoughts of someone frantic and panicking. Melody's heart started racing when she realized this person knew of them and was not expecting Ezra and Melody to show up in Athelage. They were nervous and worried about their own safety now that they had arrived. The person knew Carson. Melody was certain they were trouble. She should have stuck around to listen for more, but she panicked too!

Returning to her own thoughts and her own mind, she jumped out of the chair and grabbed Ezra.

"Ez, I heard someone! They were thinking about Carson and they know we are here! They were nervous and panicking. This must be the guard that King Ezra is looking for!"

69

"Who was it?" Simon was the first to ask as he quickly jumped to his feet.

"Well, I'm not sure," Melody was embarrassed that she didn't know more, but she still didn't have full control over this power of hers. She wasn't sure how far away the person had been and really couldn't tell them anything other than that short glimpse into their thoughts.

"It's okay Mellie," Ezra tried to reassure her because he knew she was disappointed in herself. "At least we know that we were right all along. Someone inside the palace is definitely working with George Carson."

Francesca looked at Simon with concern and said, "And they know they're here."

Chapter Eight: A Safe House is a Nightmare

"We have to do what is necessary to keep them safe! It isn't any different now than when they were babies, Kasiah," King Ezra whispered curtly to Queen Kasiah.

They were having what appeared to be a heated discussion, but they didn't want the children to know so they were whisper yelling at each other. It was clear that King Ezra suggested something that Queen Kasiah was not willing to do, but he thought it was for the best in order to continue to keep his children safe. After hours with the guards, he still did not know who was working against them, and he was not happy to hear that Melody had heard someone inside the palace that was connected to George Carson.

King Ezra and Queen Kasiah finally turned to the rest of them. Kasiah gestured for Ezra and Melody to sit down next to her on the large white sofa. Her hazel eyes which had been filled with so much joy only hours earlier were now filled with sadness. The tears welled up in her eyes threatening to streak down her cheeks. She looked to her husband to speak for her because she just didn't have it in her.

"We haven't received the news we had hoped for today. There is still so much that we just don't know. I think it would be best if we send you to a house just outside of the kingdom walls until we can be sure you will be safe," King Ezra spoke matter of factly as he attempted to keep his own emotions in check. Surely he didn't want to send his children away again after finally getting them back. But he wanted to be sure they would be safe, and right now he just wasn't sure they were.

Ezra nodded in understanding and Melody bowed her head so he wouldn't see her tears. Simon and Francesca worked out the details with the King and Queen. No one would know where they were including the council. Queen Kasiah had put great faith in them by

71

even telling them that her children had returned, but they had agreed no one should know where they were from now on. Simon and Francesca would stay with the children to continue to protect them.

"We could help," Melody whispered timidly to her mother.

"Melody, I know you want to help. And I know your abilities will one day be exceptional. But right now it isn't worth the risk to you and your brother. You are still learning and this is all so new to you. We will get this all fixed and you will be back with us very soon," she promised as she brushed Melody's hair from her eyes and placed her hand on her cheek.

Melody nodded her head to show she understood, but she was disappointed. They would be leaving the palace before even spending one night as a family. She wanted to be useful and just wanted to be given a chance to use her power to help them all. Melody was certain that she would be able to tell which guard had something to hide if she was just given a chance. Francesca agreed.

"We will figure this out and be back together again very soon. I promise," Queen Kasiah declared trying to reassure her children.

"Your majesty, I really don't want to step on your toes, but I really feel like Melody has such a wonderful gift. I think she really could help if given the chance. It might be good for them to also feel useful. You should really consider it," Francesca addressed the Queen carefully as she was not sure how she would react.

"If she's right, it could help us turn this thing around quickly. We have known someone here was not to be trusted for so long and haven't made much headway. Let's try it," King Ezra agreed.

Ezra and Melody followed King Ezra and his head Dragon Warrior, Magnus, to the dungeon below the palace. Magnus was practically a giant. He didn't speak but he seemed happy to see the prince and princess again. He wore a white tunic under chainmail and leather pants. He had a sword around his waist along with a magic wand. He led the way down a set of stone stairs deep under the palace into a stone basement like dungeon. The stairs opened up to a large room with a hallway at the back. Down the hallway, there was a row of dark cells. It smelled musty and wet in the dungeon, but besides the few guards under suspicion, the cells were empty.

"Stay here, I will bring the men in," Magnus directed.

Ezra, Melody and the King waited in the large room while Magnus brought in three guards from the cells. The guards looked disheveled and heartbroken to be assumed a traitor. When they stopped in front of the King, all three began trying to speak in their defense but Magnus directed them to be quiet. As they stood there silently in chains, Melody began her relaxation technique. She breathed deeply and concentrated on extending her mind out toward the people standing in the room. It was like removing her own consciousness and trying to place it in their minds instead. At first, there was a lot of noise. That was to be expected with so many of them in the room with her. She tucked her hair behind her ears and let out a deep breath as she narrowed in on each voice inside of her head one by one. Picking through them she could easily tell which one belonged to whom.

"You!" she pointed to the man on the far right. He was wearing the same chainmail, tunic, and pants as Magnus. His dark hair was slicked back away from his face. The man didn't seem to be acting any different than the others, but Melody heard what he was really thinking.

He looked at her quizzically waiting for her to continue. But she did not say anything for a moment, and she continued to listen into his thoughts. He hated her. He hated them all so very much. The hate was spewing from his thoughts like a fountain he could not control. He knew what she could do with her powers, but there was no disguising that much anger and disgust in his mind.

"This man hates you. He hates all of us very, very much," Melody turned to King Ezra.

"Take him away, Magnus!"

"Well done, Princess," Magnus nodded his head at her with a smile on his face.

Melody could tell King Ezra and Magnus were both proud of her and it felt so good to help. But King Ezra still felt it was best that they leave the palace. They had apprehended one threat, but it was hard for them to tell who might know they were there already. This guard, Russ, may have already alerted his companions, and the King was not going to take any big risks when it came to their safety.

As soon as it was dark, the four friends left the palace disguised as normal people from Veya. Even Francesca wore bright colors to fit in when she usually stood out. They made their way out of town as quickly and quietly as they had entered earlier that same day without the use of magic at the Queen's insistence. She was worried that someone might be able to track their movements from the palace if they used magic, especially if changelings were indeed involved. It was a short hike in the opposite direction they had come from to the safe house. This time the journey did not take them uphill and Melody didn't struggle as much to keep up.

They followed a trail made in the dirt instead of the main road although it was difficult to see in the dark. As they walked, Ezra and Melody were surprised to see cars speeding down the road nearby. They seemed like ordinary cars and nothing like magic. However, the street lights that lined the nearby highway overpass seemed to be floating above the pavement high in the air without anything suspending them there. Melody noticed an occasional glowing bug and even in the dark, she could tell the grass around them was bright green.

"Is that it?" Ezra asked after they had been walking for about a half an hour. He pointed to a row of houses ahead of them. The houses were lined up on the side of the dirt road, and they were all quiet. Simon led the group to the last house and used the key he was given to get them inside quickly. Although the area seemed abandoned, he didn't want anyone to spot them loitering around outside.

The house was a small brick house. It was dark and bare. Francesca worked quickly to start a fire and light the candles around the room using a spell. As soon as she had waved her wand, a fire was roaring in the stone fireplace. Simon stayed perched at the front door looking out the window making sure they were not followed from the palace in Veya. When they could see better, Ezra looked around at the sparse furnishings. There appeared to be two beds in a room at the back of the house off of a small kitchen. There was running water but no electricity.

"This area has been abandoned for years. The people that lived here moved into Veya when the highway was built like many others did. It used to be part of another kingdom, but years ago all of this part of Athelage was taken over by King Ezra I. Under one ruler now, the people have more freedoms and enjoy being inside the walls of the kingdom. They feel safer that way. It is exciting, beautiful, and full of all kinds of magic tech you can't get anywhere else," Francesca explained.

"So, there used to be more than one king in the western part of Athelage?" Ezra was curious now.

"Exactly. Before King Ezra I there were four separate kingdoms of magicians. Over time, he acquired them all from one way or another. With Lukten, the king passed away without an heir. King Ezra used that opportunity to take over the kingdom for his own. The people there loved him and were glad to have him. It wasn't like a war or

74

anything like what happens in your world. King Ezra I gained Valen when he married their princess. Many years later, he took power of Horen when their King went crazy and disappeared."

Francesca and Simon continued to share details about the first King Ezra's rule while they all sat on a dusty couch together facing the window to the dirt road. They were all too worked up to get any sleep and Ezra was eager to learn as much as he could about their history. It was exciting to imagine one day being the King of Athelage and all the kingdoms. It would be important for him to know whatever he could learn about these other villages too.

Eventually, they all fell asleep except Francesca. She sat there alone in silence watching the sunrise in peace. She was worried what the day was going to bring, but she knew she was prepared for anything. She felt honored that the King and Queen trusted her to help protect their children, and she really liked them. Most of her life she had trained to protect Veya and the responsibility of caring for the prince and princess was huge for her. Growing up she had prayed for an opportunity to prove herself like this, and she was not going to fail. While they all slept, she used the quiet time to try to really evaluate her current situation and what their next move should be.

"Simon," Francesca shook him gently to wake him. "We need to talk."

Quickly realizing that he had fallen asleep while he should have been guarding the children, Simon rubbed his hands on his face and rose from the couch. He was quiet so that he wouldn't wake Ezra and Melody next to him. Francesca led him into the back room so they could talk.

"We need a plan. You and I know that Melody and Ezra are not going to be happy just sitting around here hiding out for days or possibly weeks. They want to be involved. They want to help. And what if someone finds us here? What are we going to do?"

"Right," Simon nodded and thought for a moment. Francesca was right. Who knew how long they would have to hide here. The children had been in hiding for 10 years and that hadn't been long enough. Simon wiped his glasses on the corner of his shirt while he paced the room in thought. Their goal was to keep the children a secret, hidden away and safe. But the kids would want to help find whoever was responsible. How could they do both?

"We can try to distract them with a little exploration and storytelling for a bit," Simon finally suggested.

This wasn't a half bad idea. They were in a pretty remote area. It wouldn't hurt to let the kids check out the woods nearby and the other empty houses. They could tell them more about the different magic abilities and about their ancestors. There was so much that they didn't know and Francesca could tell them. Would they go for it though?

While Ezra and Melody slept, Francesca snuck out of the house to gather some supplies they would need. She visited a market in a small village nearby for food and a few extra sets of clothes. She even stopped in the village's library to collect some history books as part of the plan to distract Ezra and Melody. She returned to the house before they even noticed she was gone.

It took Ezra a few moments to remember where he was when he first opened his eyes. He looked around the small, dusty room until his eyes spotted Francesca at the window. Simon was in the small kitchen area prepping food and his sister was asleep sitting up on the old couch next to him. Gently, he stood up from the couch trying not to disturb her. Ezra joined Francesca at the window to investigate the area. It all looked so different in the daylight. He could see the houses across the small road and down the street. They were all exactly alike. They seemed to be in a sort of small, abandoned subdivision. The grass in the yards was all overgrown and the shrubs were taking over. Some of the houses had boarded up windows and sagging roofs. From this window, Ezra couldn't see the busy highway that he knew was nearby, but he could hear the cars as they drove by.

"It's really quiet here," Simon said as he handed Ezra a paper plate of fruit.

"So what do we do now?" Ezra asked taking a bite of food.

"Today we teach," Francesca smirked.

After Melody and Ezra had eaten and cleaned up, Francesca started her lessons. They sat outside to feel the fresh air. Simon hoped the new and beautiful scenery wouldn't distract them too much as he caught himself staring at the brilliant blue sky. Francesca explained to Melody and Ezra how each magician was usually born with a primary ability that was just a part of who they were. These abilities included things like mind magic, physical strength, fire power, ice magic, water abilities and even the ability to control others. This ability couldn't be taught, but they could get better at using it with practice. Some magicians even had secondary abilities that weren't usually as strong. She explained that it was perfectly normal for magicians to only have the one magic ability though. Simon also told them about the different spells that could be taught. Most magicians could do basic spells using a magic wand with proper instruction. These spells included things like freezing time, traveling short distances, moving objects, transforming things, and so much more. Spells could also come in handy during battles. Ezra wondered when they would get a magic wand like Francesca had.

"It is common for members of the royal family to be skilled in even three or more lines of abilities naturally," Francesca said excitedly. She went on to explain some of the magic abilities that past Kings had shown. It was interesting to hear about their ancestors from Francesca. She knew so much. Simon added in parts of stories that he had heard over time. He also seemed to know a lot about the Dragone family history. It was as if he had spent years studying them.

"Is it common for elves and dwarves to have the same abilities as magicians?" Ezra asked.

Francesca explained that elves and dwarves were often born with different natural abilities as well. Dwarves did not practice the art of spells like the magicians and elves did. They relied more on their born abilities and strength. Elves were also masters of creating potions of all kinds.

"It must have been incredible growing up here with all of this," Melody wondered how she might be different if she had known about magic all of her life. How could that change a person?

"Magic is an amazing gift that I do not take for granted after seeing the way the normal humans live," Francesca laughed as she used her magic wand to change a patch of unruly grass into beautiful red roses. "Magic can be a beautiful thing, but there are consequences. Many of us here don't fully understand that since our dominions have been in harmony for so long. But there is a dark side of magic that I hope your people do not have to see anytime soon."

Melody and Ezra agreed that it would be best for the people of Veya not to see the darkness that was looming over them. Ezra hoped they could protect them from it and rid Athelage of the evil before anyone was hurt.

After a full day of learning and practicing their magic with Francesca and Simon in the small front yard of the abandoned house, Ezra and Melody were exhausted. They all went back into the house and ate when it became dark. Ezra and Melody fell asleep together on the small couch while Simon and Francesca took turns keeping watch for the night.

It was dark, the only light coming from a small fire in the fireplace and the moon shining through the dusty front window of the house. Ezra and Francesca had gone to search the surrounding homes for lanterns and other discarded supplies, leaving Melody safe with Simon. But when Melody came out of the bathroom she didn't see Simon. She quickly and silently scanned the room with her flashlight. When she didn't see him, she focused her mind on the outside world. Poof, he was just gone and she couldn't feel his presence. He wouldn't just leave her here alone, unprotected. Something felt very wrong. Melody began to panic. She couldn't recall hearing any noises while she was in the other room for just a brief moment.

"Simon?" she called out but there was no answer.

She closed her eyes and let out a deep breath, focused all of her concentration outward as Francesca had taught her. Scanning the house with her mind, she came up empty. Melody then pushed her consciousness outside of the four walls and toward the dark, dirt road. Her skin began to prickle as the hair on her arms stood. She felt something but didn't hear it. Something was out there. And...

BANG, before she had a chance to determine what that something was, her world went black with a sharp blow to the back of her head.

Melody jumped to her feet suddenly with a scream startling them. Ezra turned to her now standing in front of the couch where moments ago she had been sound asleep. She was out of breath and seemed dazed.

"What was that for?" Ezra tilted his head and raised his brows in confusion.

They all stared at her waiting for an explanation.

"I was attacked! It...was... night..." Melody spoke between large gulps of air as she tried to catch her breath. "It felt so real..." she sat down shaking her finger in the air asking them for just a minute to catch her breath first. Then she continued.

When Melody finished telling the others about her dream, they all were silent. Each of them understood that this was serious and that they would not be safe here for long. The last time Melody had a dream like this, it had come true. Simon was the first to break the silence.

"We cannot keep you here. And somehow we need to let the King and Queen know that we have left. I am certain it will not be long before they have this all straightened out and come looking here for us."

"Maybe one of us should go back to the palace? Maybe they have another safe place we could stay?" Francesca suggested.

They all appeared to be thinking this over. How would they decide who would go back to the palace alone?

"I have a better idea," Ezra said.

So it was all decided. Francesca was to go halfway back toward the palace before using her phone to call the Queen and King. There was minimal risk in using it because things like this weren't tracked here like they were in Ezra and Melody's world. Wizards or magicians were more likely to trace the use of magic than a phone call. She would call them and tell them they were leaving, and then they would be able to call her when things were safe. While she was making her trip, Simon, Ezra, and Melody would start walking in the other direction. This would put a little distance between them while Francesca made her call, just to be safe. They would then walk all day and meet up with Francesca in Horen, a small northern village.

"I know it still seems like a big risk to be in the open, but trust me. It has to be better than what will happen if we stay here. I think we need to move quickly," Francesca tried to reassure Melody.

Melody and Ezra agreed it was the best plan. They all quickly gathered their things and Simon decided to check out some of the houses for abandoned supplies before they left. Francesca hugged Melody tight saying goodbye. Ezra pulled Francesca away from the others to say goodbye.

"Be careful." He said as he squeezed her shoulders tightly. "And don't take too long. We will all be worrying every second you are away from us."

Ezra had grown fond of Francesca. She was strong and smart. He liked having her around to help keep his sister safe. He hoped that one day he would be as skilled as she was. In a way, he looked up to her. It

79

was nice to have a friend when his whole world changed in such a short time. He would worry about her being out on her own when they didn't know who was coming for them.

Chapter Nine: Friend or Foe

Melody and Ezra changed into clean tunics and pants that had come from the palace. Francesca wore her usual all-black attire. She had black leather boots up to her mid-calf and tight black pants. Her black top had a hood she only wore when she was trying to be discreet. A belt around her waist carried a small pouch and her wand. Francesca smoothed her long black hair into a high ponytail so that it was out of her face like she usually did. Simon had also appropriated a few articles of clothing from the palace that he now put on. The tunic he wore was tight around his biceps and chest. He was bulging out all over the place. Ezra tried not to laugh when he saw him in his new clothes because the timing just wasn't right for picking on him. Normally he would have been down to give him a hard time for his choice in clothing, but this wasn't a normal day back home.

As Francesca began her walk south back toward the palace, Ezra and Melody accompanied by Simon, the nonmagical librarian, made their way to an unknown village following a dirt road. As far as Ezra could see it was just a dirt path, some trees, and flat fields of bright, unfamiliar flowers. They were far from the sounds of buzzing traffic from the highway now, and the only sounds they heard were their own footsteps and the occasional sounds from the foreign wildlife. It was hard to keep walking when the desire to stop and enjoy all of the beautiful new things was so strong, but they continued on in silence each of them wanting to make it to safety before the sunset left them in the dark unknown territory.

The group had not been walking for more than 20 minutes when Simon stopped them. They could still see the teeny tiny houses they had left in the distance when Simon said he needed to stop in the woods to check out his map and find a place to relieve himself.

"Come on, there is no one around. We have not seen anyone at all. It will just take me a minute," Simon persuaded.

Reluctantly Ezra followed but Melody was glad to get a minute to sit. They sat in the shade just inside the cluster of trees off the dirt road to look over the map while Simon walked a little further into the trees out of sight. Melody got distracted by all of the beautiful things inside the woods. The vibrant colors surrounded them and filled her with peace, an overwhelming kind of calm. She could hear the melodic sounds of a stream in the background and the birds sitting high in the giant trees above their heads.

"Wow! Look at the bird!" she pointed to a bold yellow bird as small as a hummingbird that was perched on a low bush a couple of feet from where she was sitting.

Ezra enjoyed the wildlife just as much even though he pretended to be unimpressed.

"Could you imagine growing up with all these beautiful things? No wonder no one wants to leave." Melody asked him.

The bird flew away quickly letting out a shrill squawk at the sound of a branch breaking directly behind where they were sitting. Before she could turn, Melody was grabbed from behind. She tried to yell out for Ezra or Simon but some kind of magic was muffling the sound of her voice and squeezing her so tight she couldn't move her arms. The more she tried the harder it was to fight back or even breathe. Her brother lay next to her in the grass unconscious. He had clearly been knocked out by a blow to the back of the head. She screamed out for him and fought with all of her might to get away from their attackers but it was no use. Every time she tried to move she felt like she was being pressed by a ton of bricks. A man wearing a black hooded robe picked up a lifeless Ezra and threw him up over his shoulder without making a sound. Another man dressed in the same black robe, spun Melody around to face him as he flung her up over his shoulder and carried her away. It was hard to make out the man's features through the low hanging hood, but Melody thought she saw the same glowing eyes she had once seen on George Carson. He was laughing as Melody continued to try to fight and scream. Melody felt completely powerless as she was thrown into the back of a four-door car parked only a few feet up at the edge of the woods. How did they not see the car before they entered the woods she thought. She could have sworn they were being more cautious. The second robed man tossed Ezra into the car next to her and climbed into the driver's seat. Melody noticed a tattoo on his arm of a black dragon head when the sleeve of his robe slid up.

Melody scanned her eyes around the car looking for some clue as to who these men were and what they were going to do next while the two men sat silently in the front seat. They weren't moving and time seemed to stand still. Without Ezra to help her, she felt hopeless. Why were they just sitting here still? And then Melody saw Simon running up from the trees. Panic rose inside of her like a volcano about to erupt. If Simon came running up here unarmed and with no magic, he was surely going to get hurt. He looked tough, but he wasn't going to be able to help them, and she couldn't bear the thought of someone else being hurt because of them. But then he opened the front passenger side door and slid in with the two robed men like he belonged there. Panic was quickly replaced with rage and confusion. Melody realized now by the wicked smile that Simon wasn't ever in any danger, and he was the enemy all along. This man that they had trusted, her parents had trusted all of these years, the King and Queen now trusted, was the unknown evil they had always been running from. He had been there all along. He had always known where they were and who they were, hadn't he?

"Ready boss?" the driver said in a rough voice as he turned to Simon.

"Let's get out of here before that brat catches up to us," Simon replied as he looked out the window to be sure Francesca wasn't in sight.

And just like that Melody lost all hope. If they all could be so easily manipulated by Simon, she had no hope of getting away. She had no hope of being reunited with the King and Queen or her parents. She had no hope of saving their kingdom if the Black Dragons intended on hurting it. They had all trusted Simon without any doubt. Now what?

The car whirred and hissed to life and they were magically transported to another location. It felt very much like jumping through a portal, Melody thought. She tried to look around but without being able to move her head and body around, all she could see was a leaning shack with boarded up windows surrounded by a field of giant sunflowers. The sun was beginning to set in the distance, and it wouldn't be long before Francesca realized they hadn't made it to safety. She would be searching for them in no time. Melody knew deep in her gut she needed to make a run for it as soon as she could, but she was still under some kind of spell keeping her from being able to move or even make a sound. Her older, stronger, braver brother was still

83

knocked unconscious next to her on the seat. If only he would wake up, she was sure that they could get away and that no spell could contain his power. That's when it dawned on Melody for the first time to test her own power. She wasn't sure what good it would do but maybe she could at least figure out what they planned to do to her, and if her parents were safe. Why hadn't she thought to test her powers on Simon before now? Now she was so mad at herself for never reading his thoughts and catching on to him long ago. Angry tears ran down her cheeks. Melody was just so mad at Simon and at herself for blindly trusting in him. How could she have let this happen to them? How useful was her power if she never even used it to catch the bad guy?

But Melody soon found her perfect opportunity to snoop through their minds when Simon and his goons got out of the car. They were standing huddled at the back of the car having a very intense conversation. She knew she needed to figure out what they were planning next. This might give her and Ezra an advantage. She pushed through all of her fear and her frustration. Melody focused all she had on the thoughts in Simon's head. She tried so hard she thought her own head might explode. Recalling the steps that Francesca had taught her, Melody tried to relax by slowing her breathing almost like she was meditating; her consciousness leaving her mind and extending out to the others outside of the car.

"The wizard will be pleased we were able to pull this off. Now we have the magic doorknob. We just need to wait for everyone to get here so we will be ready for the attack. Let's just hope this cell holds them long enough," Simon's thoughts came into her mind crystal clear. Melody panicked. Why was the magic doorknob that Sarah had given them so important to them? Where were they planning to attack? She still felt so confused by his scattered thoughts and they didn't help her with a plan to get out of there at all. Melody could feel the anticipation and blood lust coming off of the two hooded goons. They were ready for a war. They didn't have any thoughts except for obedience to Simon. She wasn't sure why these things wanted to help him so badly. What did they have to gain from any of this? Melody cried silently in the back of the car hopeless, powerless, and defeated until the men returned to the car and dragged her and Ezra out. Melody imagined herself screaming and fighting and getting away or Ezra waking up and taking them all out at once. But none of that happened.

The shack was dark and dirty inside. It smelled like rotting food and mildew. There was a thick layer of dust on every surface and cobwebs were claiming every nook and cranny. No one had been here in a very long time. Well, there goes any hope of someone coming home to find them and rescue them, Melody thought. As she watched the group working, it was clear that Simon was the leader. He watched as the two goons carried Melody and Ezra to a room in the back of the shack. There was barely any light coming in through the boarded up windows. Silently, they locked them inside of a small metal cell and left. As soon as they were gone, Melody felt the control over her body lift. She moved her head side to side to loosen her neck muscles and raced to Ezra's side. He was still unconscious lying on the dirty cell floor. She noticed dried blood on his neck as she lifted his head up into her lap.

"Ezra. Ez. Come on wake up. Please wake up. Ez I need you!" Melody cried. Ezra's eyes fluttered under his pink lids for a moment before they opened.

"Mel, what happened?" Ezra sat up slowly rubbing the back of his head where his blonde hair was matted with blood as he scanned the room.

Melody quickly told Ezra what happened in the woods and what she knew about where they were now. Ezra was furious that Simon would do this to them. After all this time, they had trusted him. He was like a part of their family ever since he could remember. All he could think about was getting out of here and tearing him to shreds for what he did. It took Ezra a few tries to get to his feet with the room spinning around him. Melody was worried he had a concussion and tried to get him to sit.

"I'm fine. We have to get out of here before they come back," Ezra said as he inspected the rusty cell they were now locked inside. The room was growing darker by the minute and soon they wouldn't be able to see to find their way out.

"Screw it!" Ezra said as he threw everything he had at the door of the cell. At first, nothing happened but after a few more tries, he felt the door start to give.

"It's working!" For the first time since they were grabbed, Melody felt her hope returning.

But that tiny glimmer of hope they were now feeling would be fleeting. The next time Ezra hit the door he was thrown across the cell into the wall by a strong magical force and a bright flash of blue momentarily lit the room. Dust fell from the ceiling and the metal on the cell groaned.

"Ezra, are you okay?" Melody helped him back to his feet worried about his already injured head.

"What was that?" he carefully investigated the cell door and saw that the magical blast had returned the cell door back to its original shape.

"We're never going to get out of here!" Melody wailed.

"Calm down. Let's think this through." Ezra sat staring puzzled at the door completely lacking any other plan to get out.

All this power, and here they were stuck in a magic cell who knows where. All of the light had left the room making it even more challenging to plan an escape. Ezra and Melody sat silently in thought while their eyes adjusted to the darkness. Ezra had to get his sister out of here. He just had to find a way. She was losing hope and he was desperate to save her.

Out of the silence, Ezra thought he heard footsteps. They were very light steps that couldn't have belonged to the three large men. He cocked his head toward the door and tapped Melody's shoulder. She nodded letting him know that she heard it too. Panic started to rise inside of her as the floorboards outside of the room creaked. Melody's heart raced in her chest as she prepared for what might be on the other side of the door. When the door to the small bedroom they were locked away in slowly opened, bright light from a flashlight flooded the darkness.

"Ezra! Melody!" They heard Francesca's voice before they could actually see her behind the blinding light of the flashlight in her hand.

She worked quickly to get the cell door open using her magic wand.

"I don't know how much time we have," she said as she brushed hair out of her face and continued to work at the door.

"How did you find us?" Ezra asked.

"When I made it away from the safe house to make the call, I saw a car coming down the dirt road. It was very unusual so I started walking back. I was just a little passed the safe house when I saw the car parked in the distance. I knew something was wrong. By the time I made it to the grove of trees where the car had been, it was gone, but I found Simon's bag left by the edge of the trees. Where is he? Is he okay?" Francesca shined the flashlight around looking for her uncle. Melody hesitated to answer because she wasn't sure how she was going to tell Francesca that he wasn't who he pretended to be. She wasn't even sure what Simon was really up to and how to explain it.

"Simon helped the guys bring us here. It was all a trick," Ezra didn't hesitate. He didn't really care about how it sounded, Francesca needed to know the truth so they could be on their way again as far from this place as possible.

Francesca looked stunned and disappointed, but they didn't have much time left to chat. She got the door opened and the three of them were off. Once they were outside of the shack, Ezra picked up Melody, and they followed Francesca as she raced through the field of flowers in the dark. Francesca stopped and ducked down at the edge of the field. She wasn't very tall, but she moved very quickly on her short legs.

"We have to stay hidden until we get closer to the village so it's best if we don't take the main road. It's going to be hard to find our way in the dark so stay close," she said switching off the flashlight for better cover in the dark.

They moved at a slower pace and Melody was able to keep up on her own two feet this time. They ducked through fields and trees keeping themselves hidden and as quiet as possible. Francesca, Ezra, and Melody walked on like this for what seemed hours. The further away from the shack they got, the safer they all felt. Just before the sun began to rise, Melody spotted the clay and metal roofs of houses on the horizon. She couldn't help but smile as she thought of finally reaching safety again. They had been out here in what felt like a war zone all night filled with fear. Her feet were tired, sweat covered every inch of her, and her mind was racing. She had been trying too hard to be alert to any sound or movement around them while also trying to work out some sort of plan. All they knew now was that they had to make it to the village of Horen. But then what would they do? Where did Simon and his goons go when they left the shack? Were the King and Queen safe still?

"Are you sure it will still be safe here now that Simon knows our plan?" Ezra whispered to Francesca.

"Horen is home to one of the most powerful wizards this side of Athelage. We'll be safe under his protection the second we step across that border."

Francesca sprinted across the open field until she reached a tall brick building that resembled an old church with a bell tower and stained glass windows. There was even a large cross on the side wall. It looked like the oldest building in the small village as most of the houses looked new or recently renovated with their metal rooftops and fresh paint.

Ezra could feel the magic protection radiating from it like the heat coming off an engine.

"We're here," she said as she let out a deep sigh and sat down leaning against the back wall of the building.

She took off her boots and stretched her legs out trying to ease the tension from walking all night. Ezra and Melody sat down on either side of Francesca and did the same. Francesca decided that it would be best to wait here until they heard the sounds of people. The town was likely all still in bed and she didn't want to draw attention to Ezra and Melody by rousing the whole town at dawn. They would then find this wizard, Calpenitin, and try to find out where Simon was now.

"Get a little rest while you can," Francesca said.

There was no way Ezra was going to be able to sleep, but Melody felt her eyelids being pulled closed by imaginary weights since the second she sat down and took her shoes off.

"Maybe just for a minute," she replied as she rested her head on her backpack next to her and closed her eyes.

Calpenitin, the wizard, looked much like Melody would expect a very powerful wizard would look. He wore a long gold robe embroidered with intricate designs of emerald. They looked like distant galaxies sewn into gold. He had a long black beard and long black hair sprinkled with gray. Calpenitin lived inside the large stone building Melody assumed was a church. His voice was loud and deep and he had a very serious look to him. He sure didn't seem like someone you would want to cross. Francesca seemed to have a sort of teacher-student relationship with him from the way they communicated.

"Never trust the outsiders!" He said. "Haven't I always told you that? Have you learned nothing? He is envious of what you have and wants to take it for himself!" He boomed.

Francesca nodded in agreement. She had been devastated to learn about her uncle's hijinks and now she seemed more embarrassed by her own mistake in trusting him. They followed the elderly wizard down a deep hallway and a stone staircase into a basement. It opened up into a large room filled with wrestling mats, targets, punching bags, and other exercise equipment. The room was enormous and seemed to run under the entire village.

"What is this place?" Ezra asked Francesca as he picked up a bow from a weapons stand.

"This is the fighter's gym. Calpenitin teaches other students here. He teaches basic fighting skills and magic to students who travel from all over. Most of them stay in his home or with other families inside Horen. Yet another reason we should feel safe here," Francesca smirked.

After hearing this, Ezra was ready to put his guard down a little and get some rest. Calpenitin showed them to a row of cots at the back of the room where they could rest a bit while he went to form a plan with Francesca and the fighters of Horen.

Chapter Ten: A Prince, a Princess, a Wizard, and Their Army

"Hope you are well rested. There is much that needs to be done now," Calpenitin, the wizard of Horen, said to Francesca as they followed him into a large room that resembled the sanctuary of the church. Young men and women all in black were lined up in tight uniformed rows just inside the room. There must have been about 50 trained fighters standing there. They did not move a muscle when Ezra and Melody walked past them, just like military soldiers.

"I was thinking about it, and I think we need to hunt down Simon and whoever attacked the Prince and Princess in the woods," Francesca stated.

"Thank you, Francesca, for all that you have done to protect our realm. But we have a better plan in motion. The King and Queen need protecting. They do not know who they can trust at this time, but I know that they can trust our fighters. No one else would show the same diligence and dedication. We need to send these men and women there today. The royal family will be safe under their protection. Then we will decide what to do about this group of traitors. Maybe we will get lucky and our enemy will come to us as well," Calpenitin spoke in such a way that there was no room for negotiation or discussion. It was clear to Melody and Ezra that his word was final, and they would all be heading to the palace together, immediately.

After the wizard finished speaking, there was a rush of activity as the group prepared to leave. It would be dark soon, but Melody and Ezra were equipped with a fresh change of clothes and a magic orb light. The lights would hover just in front of them lighting the way as they headed back toward the palace. They changed quickly into matching black leggings and form-fitting black tanks made for a fighter. They were surprisingly comfortable, light, and fit exactly to their size. The walk would be long, but this time they were flanked by all sorts of magic and strength. Ezra and Melody didn't feel afraid this time. They were ready to meet Simon and fight to save their kingdom. A change of clothes and the added fighters did so much for their motivation. Melody was ready to take out all of that anger she felt and she wasn't going to let Simon see her cry this time!

The fighters were assembled near the town line when Melody and Ezra joined them in their new gear. This time they all bowed down to their Prince and Princess as Melody and Ezra joined Francesca and the wizard. It felt empowering to Ezra to see the respect these people had for him when they didn't know him. They were ready to fight for him and his sister and without question; these trained magicians would give up everything for the cause. It was what they chose to do with their life. It was an honor like Ezra had never felt before. Winning the high school state championship couldn't even compare to this.

"Ezra, Melody, I'd like you to meet Kye. This is my older brother," Francesca introduced them to a tall, lean fighter in all black. He wore his long black hair in a knot high on his head. The sides of his head where it was shaved were covered in tattoos that looked like ancient symbols and signs. Francesca had told Ezra about the tattoos before so he knew they represented the magic abilities Kye had learned. He had dark green eyes and the same stern look on his face that Francesca often had.

"It is an honor to meet you," Kye bowed in front of them to show his respect.

"Kye will be leading the fighters. He is very skilled and as one of the oldest fighters here in Horen, he is well respected. No one is better for the job." Melody could tell that Francesca was very proud of her brother and his accomplishments with the fighters guild.

It appeared like each fighter wore some sort of tool belt around their waist that contained different items they might need including sleek, black wands. They all wore the same black clothing that Melody and her brother were now wearing. The fighters began assembling in lines again this time behind them with Kye and Calpenitin in front. The Prince and Princess now had an army. Melody dared Simon to pick on them now!

It was nearly dusk when the caravan including 50 or more fighters lead by the powerful wizard Calpenitin, Francesca, Kye, and Prince Ezra Ezeen Dragone VII and Princess Melody Estelle left Horen.

They headed south toward the palace of Veya in silence. Each person preparing for the worst once they reached their destination. Each fighter was ready to fight to the death to protect Ezra and Melody. The anticipation hung in the air. With all of these people behind them, it was finally sinking in that they were royalty. Their lives were so important to these people that they spent years training and learning magic just for this purpose. Francesca was proud. Ezra was humbled. Melody was nervous.

The path ahead was lit by the bright glowing orbs that floated in front of them. In the light from the orbs, the caravan hardly noticed it was getting dark all around them. They walked at a steady pace. Fast enough to feel they were getting somewhere, but not so fast that Melody couldn't keep up.

"What does Calpenitin expect to find when we get to the palace?" Ezra whispered to Francesca.

"I'm not sure. But I know he is prepared for a fight. It would almost be easier if Simon was there already, wouldn't it?" She replied.

In a sense, she was right, Ezra thought to himself. If Simon was already there they wouldn't have to hunt him down or spend time waiting on edge. They could end all of this tonight. The thought got his adrenaline pumping. He was anxious to see the man who had fooled them and caused pain to his family. The man who hurt Sarah and Cooper deserved to be punished. Thinking about all they had done for him and his sister, Ezra was angry. Sarah had always treated Simon like family. And there was no reason to question his loyalty after they went missing.

As they continued the walk back to the palace, Ezra remembered times Simon had come to their home for holidays, birthday parties, and family dinners. He remembered Simon coming to his sports games with his parents. Simon used to tell him he was going to teach him how to drive in his car. He sometimes took them out for pizza and bowling so his parents could go to conferences at school or date nights. This man might have been Francesca's real uncle, but he had felt like their family too. He wondered if Francesca had any fond memories of him that she was now dealing with on her own.

"Francesca, isn't it weird?" Melody stole the words out of Ezra's mouth. He might have put it a little more eloquently, but Francesca understood what she meant.

"I guess it's really unexpected, but you probably knew him better than I did. It's not like he could come to visit, and I wasn't allowed to spend a lot of time there with him either. I wonder if that has anything to do with it."

Francesca stared off into the distance as if she were trying to put the pieces together. She was still trying to wrap her head around all of this not entirely sure why this had happened and what her uncle was hoping to achieve. What was the end game?

"You never told us how you got to live here. I mean, he said his whole family was exiled a long time ago. But if that were true, how are you here?" Ezra asked.

"Well isn't that an interesting tale," Francesca smirked. "Simon was the one who was exiled. He was probably no older than you, Ezra. He was caught using dark magic to try to summon the dead. He was up to all kinds of odd things as a kid. Caused trouble, broke rules, ran away, and that was the final straw. My grandmother, his mother, went with him when he was told he had to leave. He was stripped of all of his power and told to never return. I'm surprised the King and Queen didn't throw a fit when he returned, but then again that was so long ago that most people have forgotten and those that remember probably just thought he made a mistake. He was just a kid. My mom always talked about it like he didn't know any better. She tried to rationalize it because she loved him. I am sure others did too, but I think it's pretty clear now that he was evil then and even more so now."

"He can raise the dead?" Francesca could hear the worry in Melody's voice.

Simon didn't seem like much of a match for them with this army of fighters, but if he was powerful enough to raise the dead as a kid, who knew what he would be capable of.

"He didn't actually do it. He was just messing around with spells and trying. Plus, as far as we know, he doesn't have any magic now. I'm not sure what it would take for him to get it back, but it would be pretty difficult for him and a couple of guys to do on their own. I am sure we can stop them before he has a chance to get his powers again," Francesca explained.

Ezra could tell that Melody didn't feel as confident as she did when they had left Horen. "What about the people that he is working with? George Carson didn't seem like an ordinary kinda person. And I saw one of those other goons eyes glow just the same. There's something off about that. You said something before about changelings?" Melody said.

"Yes, we believe he is working with changelings. Changelings are lower level magicians with evil spirits. They mostly practice dark magic. You don't see many around here, but sometimes they hide in plain sight. Their true form is pretty grotesque, but they can easily manipulate your mind to make you think you see a regular human form."

"Changelings? What other kinds of dark things live here?" Ezra remembered Francesca mentioning changelings before too.

As the group continued their conversations about ogres, changelings, dark elves and other beings the kids had only read about or seen in movies, the sun had completely disappeared in the hills to their right. The glow of the orbs made it as easy to maneuver the terrain as it did during the day, and they didn't slow down. Melody focused her attention on Francesca's stories of the other regions and the other beings they might one day see. This kept her legs from feeling tired or sore. The distraction was nice to keep them from worrying about what might be waiting for them when they did reach the palace. Changelings and evil magicians could be attacking the palace or holding the King and Queen hostage as they spoke, but right now all they could do was keep walking. The rest of the caravan was silent as they walked. Melody found it so odd that these fighters didn't have anything to talk about to pass the time, but Francesca explained that it was just part of their nature to avoid small talk. They were mentally preparing for what would come next while also maintaining high alert in case of an attack on the road.

Melody felt they had been walking for hours. Kye must have sensed her pace slowing because his eyes did not leave her as they walked under the starry vast sky. He stayed very close behind Melody silently enjoying the conversation. He broke his silence to suggest they stop for a moment. Kye took a small bag of fruit out of his pack and some crackers. Francesca also had roasted chicken and cheese in her pack that she was willing to share. Ezra couldn't believe that leftovers could taste so good, but then again they had been practically starving since they arrived in Athelage a few days earlier. The rest of the caravan took the time to also refuel before they were on their way again.

"We wouldn't want to burst in the palace doors on an empty stomach. It could very well be a long night still ahead of us," Kye said to Francesca as they all readied to finish the hike.

When they reached the abandoned house where Francesca, Ezra, and Melody had slept with Simon, they knew they were getting close.

Seeing that house helped to reenergize the trio as their steps grew longer and faster. The group of fighters that followed behind them also increased their speed to match their stride without missing a step. Finally, the lights from the large village of Veya lit up the sky in the distance. As the shadowy towers of the palace came into view, the fighters began to quietly sing in unison. They sang a beautiful battle song that Francesca explained was part of their tradition. It was used to motivate and inspire them as they prepared to fight. Listening to the words of the song was inspiring and Ezra could feel his adrenaline begin to spike again. When the group began the chorus again, Ezra joined in on the singing.

"Hear our song as we march on. We do not fear any enemy that's near. Brothers and sisters, we have been waiting all of our lives for such a fight. We are the Horen fighters and we march on. We march on. Fearless and loyal, we march on. We will slay to protect our kingdom's honor. We will fight to the death for our King. So hear our song as we march on."

As they grew closer, the fighters ended their singing. Melody wasn't sure what time it was but she knew it must have been late. They didn't see anyone out on the streets inside Veya and everything was very quiet. She assumed everyone was asleep inside the village. The caravan made their way on the winding path toward the palace in the heart of the village. They passed dark stores and houses to get to the same bridge they had walked before. The guard's post was lit with large floating orbs similar to the ones they had been using that night. But there was no guard at the post. Calpenitin took a moment to speak with Kye before deciding to cross the bridge without the permission of a guard.

Chapter Eleven: Distant Places and Foreign Allies

Kye took the lead as they entered the large gilded doors of the palace single file. The entry foyer was dimly lit and there were still no guards to be seen. They all walked swiftly and quietly toward the throne room in the middle of the lower level. The palace felt very different from when they were there a few days prior. Before, there had been a lot of activity. People were busy carrying out tasks and hurrying around. Tonight, there was no sound. No one was hurrying from one room to the next. The giant throne room was dark and empty when they entered.

"Maybe everyone is asleep?" Ezra suggested, but it was more of a wish.

"But what about the guards? You would think there would be someone to stop us from just entering the palace front door in the middle of the night," Kye said.

And he was right. Ezra didn't want to think of the worst, but something was definitely wrong here. A guard should have been here and wasn't. The King and Queen should have protection around the clock and it shouldn't have been so easy for them to enter the palace the way they did.

"You stay here. I will take a handful of fighters and check around a bit," Kye said to Ezra and Melody. He spoke quietly to a few of the fighters that were gathered nearby, and they left the throne room.

Melody stayed close to Ezra and Francesca while they waited with Calpenitin and the others. The last time she had been here in this room she had been filled with so much excitement at being there and meeting the King and Queen. This time was very different. Her stomach was in knots, and she felt she just might be sick with nerves. The palace was very eerie all dark and quiet. Her eyes darted around the room looking from one corner of the giant marble floor to the other thinking maybe she saw something or heard something, but there was nothing there. She could tell that Ezra was on edge too. His hands were balled up at his sides and he kept his back to one wall so that he could see if anyone entered the room. His gray eyes hardly blinked. Francesca paced a small space of the room but stayed very close to them. She was anxious for something to happen already so she could prove herself.

Ezra felt like they had been waiting there forever when suddenly a fighter named Lenix rushed back into the throne room. The light from his orb illuminated his face as he ran to Calpenitin, the wizard.

"Sir, the palace appears to be empty, and there's a message for the Prince and Princess. Come!" Lenix gestured for Ezra and Melody to follow him out of the throne room back towards the stairs.

As they followed behind him quickly, Ezra could only hear his blood rushing. His heart was racing as they hopped up the stairs not knowing what to expect. The rest of the fighters were quickly divided up to guard the doors and finish searching the expansive palace rooms.

Ezra and Melody entered the room after Lenix. It appeared to be a private office, possibly the King's. Two fighters were waiting there standing behind a large cherry wood desk. They had concerned looks on their faces as Ezra and Melody approached.

"Here," Lenix pointed to a small, white envelope in the center of the desk with their names on it. Ezra glanced at Melody before picking up the envelope and opening it. As he opened the unsealed envelope a blue light shot up from inside. The light focused into an image. Ezra dropped the envelope back on the desk and jumped back as the image came into focus. He realized it was a holographic message from the Queen. She was dressed in a robe and looked like she had only just woken up. Her voice was shaky and hushed when she spoke.

"Children, I am afraid that the worst is happening. I hope that you are safe though I am not sure you will even see this message. If you are seeing this we are evacuating the palace immediately. I have to make this quick. The traitor locked up in the dungeon has finally revealed part of their plan. We are not safe here," she paused and looked behind her. Ezra and Melody struggled to see what she saw, but the image was fuzzy. Suddenly there was a lot of noise. With panic in her voice, the Queen continued her message, *"Something is happening! No!"* she yelled at the sound of the door being thrown open. The image of the queen looked up at where the door would have been and then quickly ended the message.

Melody was sobbing as the image of the Queen disappeared. The hope she had felt when the message began was instantly ripped away. She was left not knowing what happened after the transmission ended or who had come for the Queen. Ezra hugged his sister tightly to his chest and let her cry. He brushed her hair from her face and looked at her. He wanted to take that hurt away from her but this was their reality.

"We will find them, Mel. It's going to be okay," Ezra grabbed her face and looked right into her eyes so she would see that he meant what he said to her. He was going to fix this.

Ezra looked up at Francesca who had been standing at the office door and asked, "Now what?"

An army of fighters, a wizard, a prince, and a princess all gathered around a long table inside of a magically reinforced war room inside of the palace. They needed to plan their next moves very carefully. On the table stretched out in front of them was a map of the world. Calpenitin, the wizard, and Kye, the leader of the fighters, stared down at the map in deep thought. No one knew where Simon was now. They didn't know who was helping him, but what they thought they knew was that he was working with a terrorist group and they were after The Peacekeeper. The King would be able to help them gain one piece of the magical relic, but he would still have to obtain the other two pieces from the other dominions' possession.

"I think it's time that I reach out to the elves and the dwarves," Calpenitin said suddenly as if it only just occurred to him.

"How do we do that?" Ezra asked. He had been very curious about the other beings that inhabited this world ever since he learned of their existence. Now was the perfect opportunity to find out more about them.

Calpenitin used his wand to cast a spell. The gold wallpaper stripes on the wall where he aimed his wand now began to swirl and move like smoke. And then the spot on the wall began to look like an oval-shaped mirror. Ezra and Melody stood close behind the wizard to watch what was happening. They could see Calpenitin and themselves standing in the room reflected back at them on the wall where there once was not a mirror. Calpenitin spoke a few words under his breath until the image in the mirror changed to show a pale man with a long face and pointed ears. There was a thin silver banded crown around his head. The image was crystal clear as if the elf was actually standing right in front of them.

"Morando, can you hear me?" Calpenitin spoke loudly at the elf on the wall.

"Yes, friend. I can hear you fine. Isn't it a bit late for a chat?" The elf looked around at all of the faces in the room and then back at Calpenitin. "Something wrong?" His voice was soft and he spoke slowly, lyrically.

"Yes, your majesty. This is Prince Ezra and Princess Melody of Veya," he gestured to the siblings. "They have only just returned to our realm after an attack on them in the other lands. Their attacker has come to Veya, and we have reason to believe that he has kidnapped the King and Queen and is after The Peacekeeper," Calpenitin spoke quickly, not wanting to waste any more time.

The elf was silent for a moment. He was carefully considering the information he just received as he tucked his long, gray hair behind his ear. This was the King of the Elves, Morando with the icy blue eyes staring at them in thought.

"Sephali and I will gather our strongest and smartest. We will make way to Veya at first light. Have Brovadan do the same. This monster will not be able to hide in the shadows from us all."

"I was hoping you would say as much. Our alliance will be very beneficial as we do not know how many he has gathered behind him. We do suspect changelings are working with him."

"Prince Ezra, Princess Melody, I can't wait to finally meet you. I wish, however, that it were under happier circumstances. We will find your King and Queen." King Morando ended the conversation and disappeared as he went to do what he promised.

The wizard repeated his spell again to conjure up the King of the dwarves, Brovadan. The dwarf king's round bearded face appeared where the elf was before. His cheeks were red and his nose was bulbous. He reminded Ezra of how people described Santa in the old songs. He wore a large crown of gold and large emeralds on his head of red hair.

"Hello, wizard. What do we owe the pleasure?" Brovadan's voice was deep and raspy.

Calpenitin quickly filled the dwarf in on what had happened in Veya and requested he join the elves to help them quickly. Brovadan was angry and his face turned bright red. He yelled obscenities in a language that Melody and Ezra did not understand. Brovadan agreed to help them. He did not like the idea of Simon and changelings running amok trying to gain power and hurting Kings and Queens for it.

Dwarves, Caplenitin explained, had very short tempers, but they were very loyal to their friends. Brovadan would be an excellent ally to them at this time. The elves were a very powerful force and they were lucky to have their help, he told them. The elves would make their way from Lauraan in the morning, and the dwarves would come from the mountains of Warvelle. By afternoon they would have a full force army to handle anything that was to come. Calpenitin thought it was possible that Simon would return here for the prince and princess, especially if he did not expect the elves and dwarves to be there. But the dwarves would not be eager to sit and wait. They would be on a mission to hunt Simon and any of his followers down wherever they were hiding. The elves might insist on doing the same.

A fighter named Ruben was standing at the door waiting for Calpenitin to finish his chat with the dwarf king.

"Sir, we have found the missing palace guards. They were locked in the dungeon cells incapacitated. We have a few healers working on them now, and we should soon have some answers about what happened here tonight," Ruben explained his presence.

Calpenitin nodded and followed Ruben out of the room to be with the guards. Ezra and Melody were escorted out of the war room by two fighters. They would spend the rest of the night in their rooms for the first time. Francesca and the wizard insisted on them getting some sleep before they passed out standing on their feet.

"We don't need to be worrying about one of you passing out and hurting yourself before the fight has even begun," Kye pointed out.

Reluctantly they settled into their rooms with fighters guarding the doors and hiding in every shadow around the first floor of the palace. Francesca found a guest room down the hall from Ezra and Melody to rest up in as well. She didn't want to miss out on anything, but she knew she'd be useless if she didn't get some sleep, plus her big brother told her she had to sleep. The fighters would take shifts over the next several hours so they could rest as well. But the wizard locked himself in the war room staring at the maps and reading notes from the King's books looking for some clue about the organization working against them. Over all these years, the King must have had some ideas about who was after them or where they might hide. He was pressed to find some kind of information that he could relay to the dwarf and elf Kings when they arrived.

The palace was stirring with preparations for the day ahead when Melody came out of her room the next morning. She walked down the stairs as she watched the commotion. There were a handful of fighters in the grand ballroom practicing spells. Another group was busy preparing food. One small group of fighters was training with weapons in a room off the throne room. Melody found Ezra, Francesca, Kye, and the wizard in the war room discussing documents Calpenitin had dug up while they were sleeping. Francesca looked refreshed. Kye, on the other hand, looked like he had been up all night with Calpenitin.

"Let's catch Princess Melody up while we get some food," Kye suggested. They all made their way to the dining room down a wide hall past the throne room on the right of the main entrance. The dining room was just as large as the throne room. The shiny dark wood floor was covered with a large, gold and blue rug. The table in the center of the room was long enough to sit 50 or more people with large plush seats fit for a king. They all sat at one end of the table together after grabbing a plate of eggs and sausage from the long buffet table against the windowed wall.

"I spent the night going through the King's records and notes. I was able to piece together some of what was going on here in Veya all of those years that you two were in hiding," Calpenitin explained to Melody.

She listened intently while she shoveled giant forkfuls of eggs into her mouth. Starving and eager to hear what he had to say.

"It seems that shortly after your birth a terrorist group of sorts organized. They called themselves the Black Dragons. This group wasn't anything to be worried about at first. Mostly they made threats and met in secret. There were reports from travelers of being robbed occasionally on the main roads. They would come to Veya with messages from the group that worse was coming. Things like that. The King did not take these robbers seriously until a couple of years later. While the King was traveling to Horen for a ceremony, he himself was attacked on the roads. No one was injured. It was more of a threat and the group was not big enough to take on the Dragon Guard. But it frightened the King. He suspected that the group may have an inside man based on this attack. His comings and goings were

101

very secretive, but they somehow knew where he would be. This is when he sent you away. He didn't know who else he could trust except Sarah and Cooper."

Calpenitin paused to grab a few bites of food. Melody took it all in. If this group had been around so long, she was sure they had time to grow and expand. What kind of people would be after them?

"We all know that since you disappeared, the King and Queen made big changes around Veya. They built the walls. They trained more guards. The security became much more than it ever was. They focused more money on technology and even turned their focus away from their alliances. They encouraged their people to live within the walls of safety. They invested much more time and money into the fighters and their training in Horen even," Kye added.

"So what about the attacks?" Ezra asked.

"Honestly, there wasn't much change after you left. It seems the group went into hiding. They must have been planning, growing, and training. The King followed up on the occasional lead. It seems every so often there was an attack on a merchant for supplies or food was stolen from a storehouse. The thieves would leave behind a small coin with a black dragon head as some sort of calling card. Unfortunately, it doesn't seem like the King figured out anything about the people involved. He certainly never suspected Simon."

"Having a high-level guard working with the Black Dragons probably didn't help any of the investigations over the years. Who knows what he covered up or shared with the Black Dragons over all these years, making things rather difficult for the King," Kye added.

"And there is that! But Simon knew where we were all this time, why did it take him so long to do anything about it?" Melody asked.

"That's a good question. I'm afraid we just don't know. He was thorough, that's for sure," Calpenitin answered.

"So where is everyone else?" Ezra asked referring to all of the palace staff they had previously seen here.

"We wondered the same. Kye was able to track down some of the house employees this morning in their homes. They were already safe at home when the Black Dragons showed up last night. They didn't know anything happened, and we decided to keep it that way. Kye told them that the King and Queen were preparing for guests of extreme secrecy and asked that they not come to the palace today. We don't want to cause extreme panic across the region so it is better that they stay away for now. The guards all seem to be recovering fine, but they are all still unconscious."

"There are some caves and other abandoned places we can check, and we need to immediately secure the locations of the Peacekeeper. If he gets his hands on all of the pieces, Simon will be unstoppable." Kye added.

Melody could tell this was the part that Kye feared the most, more than what might happen to the King and Queen. She didn't know much about the Peacekeeper, but it held such great power that anyone that possessed all of the pieces would be able to harness more power than anyone else ever had. Simon would be all powerful, an unimaginable force, and an enemy like none they had ever planned to face. The fighters of Horen with the combined help of the elves and the dwarves would have to stop Simon before he could locate the three pieces.

By afternoon, they all were ready for their guests to arrive. Calpenitin had instructed a few members of the fighter's guild to meet the Kings at the gates and lead them to the palace as quickly as possible. The people of Veya were sure to see them as they paraded through the kingdom, and there would be a lot of speculation, but they were not ready to answer all of the questions. The less the people knew the better. Ezra and Melody were bursting with anticipation as they waited to meet elves and dwarves for the first time ever. They waited impatiently staring out the largest window of the third story office that faced the kingdom's gate so they wouldn't miss anything. Francesca sat near the window in a cushioned armchair waiting with them.

They didn't have to wait long before they could see horses and wagons coming over the hillside where they had climbed days before. On the backs of sleek, white horses sat tall, thin men and women all with long white hair. Their skin was pale and as their horses trodded through the gates and closer to the palace, Ezra could see their pointed ears. The elves were very poised on the backs of their giant horses. Melody couldn't wait to see the elves up close.

The dwarves were not far behind the elves. As the wizard greeted the elves in the throne room downstairs, Ezra could just barely make out the short, round dwarves making their way toward the gate on foot. They carried large bags over their shoulders and weapons that looked like clubs and axes. The dwarves moved slowly as they walked on their short legs carrying all of their things with them. There must have been 100 or 200 of them walking through the hills slow and steady. Melody waited and watched as they got closer while Ezra made his way downstairs to meet the King of the elves who had arrived as they were still watching out the window.

King Morando stood with Calpenitin in the middle of the throne room as Ezra entered the room. There were several elves standing with them as others unloaded the wagons. Ezra was in awe. He looked from one elf to another mesmerized by their perfect porcelain skin and shiny white hair. They had beautiful ice blue eyes that were startling to look at. When the elves noticed that Ezra had entered the room, they stopped talking and bowed deeply to show their respect for the prince. Ezra took their lead and bowed in return to King Morando. He smiled and nodded his head.

"Prince, it is an honor to meet you. I certainly wish that it was under different circumstances. This is my Queen Sephali," the elf King introduced Ezra to a beautiful elf wearing a pale green gown and a crown that sparkled under the giant chandeliers. Ezra still wasn't used to all the formality of being treated like royalty. Being called prince just felt strange to him. Shortly after the introductions were made, Melody joined them and received similar introductions.

The Dwarf King, Brovadan, and his people had made it to the palace by this time. They joined the growing crowd in the throne room where everyone was introduced. The dwarves were much louder and more rowdy than the elves that had arrived before them. The dwarves were small but mighty and ready for a battle. King Brovadan pulled Ezra and Melody in for a big bear hug. He told them he was so happy to finally meet them both. After everyone had a few moments to meet, Calpenitin directed them to the war room. Each king brought a handful of his people with them to discuss their plan of action.

The elves dressed in light armor and bright silver chainmail followed close behind the King carrying staffs. Their movements were very fluid like and when they walked, they looked like they were gliding slightly above the ground. The dwarf king was accompanied by rugged looking men who did not wear armor, and they laid their heavy weapons down in the foyer before following the rest of the group to the war room. They were unshaved and looked unkempt in comparison to the shiny elven knights.

Once inside the war room, Calpenitin took the lead. He explained everything that he had discovered to the Kings and showed them the maps he had uncovered. Circled on the maps were the various places they should search first, he explained. He also made sure to point out the location of the piece of the Peacekeeper hidden in Veya. Each King then presented the group with the location of their regions piece. The elf and dwarf kings had decided they did not want to travel with the pieces because there was so much they still did not know about their enemy. They felt safer keeping the pieces guarded where they had been set with great care a thousand years before.

"No threat has ever come to the Peacekeeper until now. It has been safely guarded and kept secret for all of these years. Why risk disrupting that by going to it? What if we are followed? What if that is the monster's plan all along?" King Brovadan pointed out.

"Excellent point, your majesty. If we are to keep the pieces safe, maybe leaving them is best until we find Simon." Calpenitin agreed.

The group was in agreement that they would stay away from the hidden pieces of the Peacekeeper for now and focus on finding Simon. They would start by dividing up their armies and searching the areas that were circled on the map. The fighters, elves, and dwarves all united together in the interior courtyard of the palace. Ezra and Melody joined them with the wizard. Each king divided up their people and they made plans. The palace and the courtyard were abuzz with preparations. Bags were being packed with provisions from the storerooms, maps were being analyzed, wagons were being unloaded and reloaded with proper weapons, food, and medical supplies. Magic wands were being tested, chants and battle cries erupted from the courtyard as the dwarves pumped themselves up for a fight. Calpenitin took a moment to speak with the Prince and Princess alone before it was through.

"Prince, Princess. I know that so much has happened. You have plenty to fear, but here you stand ready to help. You are very brave. We just might need your super strength and your mind reading abilities along the way so I hope that you would join me. We will make our way to the outer limits of Veya to one of the suspected hiding spots with a handful of dwarves, elves, and fighters. If there is any sign of Simon or his changelings we will be able to quickly receive aid from the rest of our friends. I don't know what we might find so we must be prepared for anything. Are you in?"

Ezra and Melody were anxious because they didn't know what to expect, but of course, they were ready to join the search. They didn't want to be sitting here in the empty palace while everyone else was out risking their lives for them. They joined the wizard in the stables to mount their horses and head out with the rest of them. The sun was setting as the army left the gates of the kingdom. People of Veya quickly left their homes to watch the magnificent scene as dwarves, elves, a long lost prince and princess, a wizard, and a bunch of young fighters rode by quickly through the streets and out into the open world. The group divided on the main road into smaller groups of roughly 20 and went in all directions on the hunt for evil hoping to return with the King and Queen.

Chapter Twelve: A Bookstore Battle

Ezra and Melody followed Calpenitin and Francesca's lead since they were familiar with the land. They rode on horseback through the beautiful landscape, flying past the stunning purple and red trees and over the hills away from Veya. They were heading toward the side of a mountain near the borderlands of Warvelle. Calpenitin had marked this location on the map because of suspicious activity over the years. The other groups would be investigating similar locations and searching for Simon and his group. The horses made impeccable timing riding faster than Melody knew was possible. This was necessary if they were planning to search all of Athelage for the King and Queen.

Calpenitin slowed as they got closer to the bottom of a rocky cliff. "We are looking for any signs of an opening, like a cave in this mountainside. Caves make great hiding places for bandits, changelings, ogres or any sort of dark soul. This could be where the Black Dragons have been hiding all of these years," he explained as he led his horse slowly along the cliff wall.

"There!" Ezra pointed to an opening about six feet in front of them as he jumped off of his horse.

The others followed his lead and dismounted from their horses. Francesca quickly got in front of Ezra to protect him from anything that might come out of the cave. She walked slowly with her arm out keeping Ezra behind her. Calpenitin performed a spell that shot a beam of light quickly inside of the mouth of the cave lighting it up only briefly for him to get a quick glimpse inside. At first glance, the cave looked empty but very deep.

Calpenitin and Francesca entered the cave opening first. It was wide enough for the group to enter two by two. Slowly and cautiously Ezra and Melody followed behind them. Francesca took out her light orb from her small satchel to light the way for them. Inside the opening, the cave continued on just barely wide enough for them to continue on two by two. The ceiling of the cave hung low causing the elves in their group to have to duck down. This would make for a slow pace. Ezra heard the sounds of water dripping inside the cave, and their footsteps echoed all around them.

About 50 feet inside the cave, it finally opened into a larger room. Stalagmites hung from the ceiling of the cave. It was dark and dank. The cave smelled like a combination of rotting meat and wet socks. Not watching her steps, Francesca nearly tripped over a pile of bones rattling them at her feet. She looked back at the group to see they were all worried now. The bones she almost fell over were human bones.

"Well that is concerning," Calpenitin said.

Just as the words were leaving his mouth the room shuttered with the sound of either giant footsteps or the steps of many. Melody grabbed Ezra's hand and stood behind Calpenitin and Francesca at the opening of the cave room. She wasn't sure what to expect next. Calpenitin was prepared, however. He knew these types of caves, and he knew the signs well. From a tunnel off the right side of the cavern, the light of a giant torch illuminated the rest of the room casting their shadows on the walls. The cave floor was littered with bones from humans and animals. There was a pile of clothing, boots, and weapons in the opposite corner. Behind the torch came a giant being Ezra did not recognize.

"Ogre!" Francesca hollered back to the rest of the group that was still down inside the tunnel. They all quickly entered the large room in order to protect the prince and princess from the threat of an ogre.

Before Ezra or Melody could react, the army of elves, dwarves, and magicians was now in front of them casting spells and waving their weapons to fend off the beast. The ogre stood ten feet tall with a thick torso. Its arms and legs were larger than Melody's entire body. It was angry that its home had been disturbed by these visitors and he was not backing down. He swung his torch like a weapon at the group, but the magicians worked fast. Before the ogre was close enough to make contact, he was frozen and blasted backward hitting the wall at the back of the cavern. The whole room shook and they were showered with rocks and dirt.

"Go!" Francesca hollered to Ezra and Melody. They didn't waste any time thinking it over and immediately headed for the exit as the ogre got back to his feet. This time Calpenitin shot him with a giant ball of energy taking him out. Giant boulders and rocks splintered from the ceiling threatening them all when the ogre's massive body hit the ground. They all ran out of the cave behind Melody and Ezra the way they had entered.

"That was close," Francesca rode with Ezra, Melody, and Calpenitin as they headed on horseback toward a portal nearby. The portal would make their traveling around Athelage faster than horseback she explained. The portals were like elevators that could take you to destinations all around this realm. There were many of these portals around Athelage hidden in caves and even in ditches on the side of the highway. Even though they were no longer used in or near Veya for safety reasons, the other groups would find similar ways of getting around the vastness of the region quickly.

"In here," Calpenitin directed the group inside of a small cave in the side of the grassy hillside. Luckily their guide knew the way because they wouldn't have been able to see the cave without knowing where to look.

They all ducked inside quickly and stepped through the portal. When they emerged on the other side, the scenery was very different. Instead of the grassy hills, Ezra and Melody saw the ocean in front of them. As far as they could see there was crystal clear water and an endless sky. It was beautiful to see just like everything else in Athelage had been. Calpenitin led the group along the shore through the golden sand. The waves lapped gently at the beach. It was almost tranquil if they hadn't been on the hunt for the monster that kidnapped the King and Queen. Ezra made a mental note that this was a place he wanted to visit after this was all over as he followed behind Calpenitin on his horse.

They rode quickly without saying a word. Towards the end of the beach, there was a small boathouse with a dock. Ezra thought the dock looked like a beautiful place to sit and enjoy the warm sun sometime, but they weren't headed there. Francesca had briefly explained to them that the place they were going was basically the end of the world. Out past that water there was nothing else. This would be a difficult place to find someone without the use of magic and portals and might be the perfect place to hide an abducted King and Queen. They rode down the beach a little further before Calpenitin dismounted his horse at the bottom of a cliff. The others followed his lead. Calpenitin took a small glass vial from his robe pocket and dabbed a little of the purple liquid on each of their wrists. The vial contained a potion that smelled a little like blueberry pancakes and latex. They all began to float quickly up the side of the cliff toward a large house on the very edge just like balloons released into the sky. Melody wasn't expecting to be floating into the sky, and as she saw her horse on the beach getting smaller she panicked. Looking at Ezra, she saw that he was thrilled to be floating which helped to ease her mind. If he was sure they weren't going to plummet to their death, then she would be fine.

The army reached the top of the cliff faster than Ezra had expected, and he was glad they didn't have to climb up on their own. The wizard's potion had been a handy time saver. As they all landed on solid ground and regrouped, Ezra noticed that it was very quiet at the top. He could barely hear the waves crashing on the beach from this height. They were all now ducking in the overgrown grass and weeds nearly 50 feet away from the house.

"Melody, I need you to try to scan the area. Can you see if you hear anyone inside the house? It'd be better not to go in there blind," Calpenitin asked.

Melody agreed to give it a try. She struggled before trying to read Simon's thoughts but maybe there was someone else around. Not sure if she wanted to hear something or not, she closed her eyes and began the steps to reach the level of concentration she needed. Hearing something inside the house could mean the King and Queen were just inside. Not hearing something could really mean a lot of things, like one that she was a failure or two that no one was here and they had to keep on hunting. She focused on her breathing and relaxation to start, and then she pushed her mind out toward the house. Melody felt her mind drape over the house like a blanket while everyone around her waited silently.

At first, Melody didn't sense anyone there. She shook her head in disappointment, but just as she was about to give up she heard a faint voice.

"Six, seven, eight, oh no there are too many of them to count. What if they kill me for being here? Oh no, I need to get out of here." Melody didn't wait to hear much more after that lone voice began panicking.

"I think there is only one. They sound scared of us, but I am not sure who it is or what they are doing. I think they are counting us," Melody rushed to tell them. As soon as the words were out of her mouth Calpenitin instructed the army to take the house. They all swarmed past Ezra and Melody working quickly to get inside the house. Ezra grabbed Melody's hand and they ran after the rest of the elves, dwarves, and magicians.

When they entered the house Melody heard the same voice yelling in an upstairs room.

"Please don't hurt me. I swear I didn't do anything to the King and Queen. I just have a message for the Prince and Princess. Please!" Ezra and Melody now stood in the doorway to the room looking at a sickly man. He was skin and bones wearing torn rags for clothing and covered in filth. His hair was thinning and spotty. No one was very scared of him. So they decided to let him deliver his message.

"The man with the changelings, he was here. A few years ago those changelings started to come here I guess because it was secluded. They stole everything I had and made me their slave. I was powerless to fight them there were just so many of them. The man came here and told me I was to tell the prince and princess that they would need to find the place where the alliance all began in order to save their parents," the man covered his face and cowered when he spoke. He was clearly terrified and had been tortured all this time.

Melody and Ezra looked to Calpenitin with uncertainty. In everything they had learned so far, they didn't know what Simon meant by finding the place where the alliance began.

"I imagine he is talking about our Peacekeeper Alliance," Calpenitin tapped his finger to his bearded chin and looked up to the sky as he tried to remember something. He turned his head from side to side in deep thought. But he just couldn't recall where this place was or if he had ever known where it was.

They needed to find this place and fast. Calpenitin decided to split the group. He sent a message to the others requesting that they join some of the fighters guild back in the Horen library where they would look for some answers there. He would lead another group including Kye, Francesca, Ezra, and Melody. This group would travel back to the book store that Sarah owned with Simon. He knew that Sarah kept many historical documents in the store. He was hopeful that between the two locations they would be able to locate some information that would be helpful. Two of King Morando's elves stayed at the house on the cliff with the injured man just in case anyone returned after they left. They were very skilled healers and would have the man back to health in no time at all.

The caravan of elves, dwarves, and fighters led by a wizard, prince, and princess rode swiftly back the way they had come. They traveled through the same portal that Ezra and Melody had arrived in only four days before. Once they were through the portal that opened up into the empty warehouse, Calpenitin cast a spell to make them all invisible to the humans. This would make it easier for them to get to the bookstore without being spotted. Their unusual clothing and features would make it hard for people not to be curious. And that would cause too many problems that they didn't need right now. It was almost sunset by the time the army made it to the bookstore led by Francesca, Ezra, and Melody. As the neared the bookstore, Melody became anxious. She felt like this might be some kind of trap to get them here, but Ezra grabbed her hand and urged her on. Her stomach in knots, she pushed herself to focus on the task at hand. She couldn't let her nerves get the best of her when all of these people were here to help them. They were brave in the face of this unknown threat. Before they entered the bookstore, Calpenitin gave Melody a moment to check out the store. She concentrated outward just like she had done so many times now. Focused and silent, she didn't hear anything inside the store. Using her power to help the group made Melody feel less anxious. She sighed with relief to learn that no one was waiting inside for them.

Ezra led the group inside the store and they divided up again. Some of the group stayed in the main room of the store and a few guarded the back door in the alley behind the store while Ezra led a few others down to the secret storage room in the basement. If there was something here that could help them, it would be locked away in this room away from the public. The file cabinets held so much information that Ezra really wasn't sure where to start. Luckily Calpenitin had just the spell to help them. He held his wand in the air and quietly chanted in another language. "Rubeus Origin Eliviate Peacekeeper".

Filing cabinet drawers began to open and pages in books started to turn on their own. And there on the long table in front of them, lay all the books with information relevant to the Peacekeeper Alliance. The group began reading through the pages of text that were open in front of them in search of where the Peacekeeper had been made. With as many people as they could spare from guarding the entries, they worked quickly to find their answer. Ezra started to get frustrated when everything he read spoke of the people involved in the alliance and how it had greatly changed the realm, but still, nothing mentioned who or where it was created.

"Here! I think I found something!" Francesca shouted. Everyone stopped reading and listened to her read aloud. "Walden the Great spent almost a century creating and enchanting the mysterious Peacekeeper. It was his life's work to see peace across the realm after years of enduring suffering at the hands of war. He hid himself away deep in the fairy wood. The cave was unsuspecting enough but contained all the right elements for creating such a masterpiece. Walden had become such a recluse that no one entered his cavern except for his best student, his own daughter. Walden created two key activated portals. These magnificent creations were second in mystery to the Peacekeeper. These keys were the only thing that allowed someone to enter his secret home in the woods where he devoted all of his time to the creation of the Peacekeeper. They have never been found.

"I don't get it. So Simon is in the fairy woods? Why would he be there?" Ezra looked at Calpenitin with uncertainty hoping he had some answers but he didn't know much more than that.

"Now I remember, I have heard of these secret keys. I am not sure I understand what Simon's plan is. I can only hope that the others have found more information in Horen. Should we get back?" Calpenitin replied.

Suddenly they heard a big crash above them. Ezra looked at Francesca as she turned to Melody. "Changelings," Melody said. And they rushed up the basement stairs.

A large group of changelings stood at the front door of the store. The changelings no longer resembled humans. There spell was gone. These changelings were horrifying. Their bodies looked withered with graying flesh hanging from the bones. It looked like someone might expect a decaying body to look with enough time. Their eyes were big yellow holes in their heads. Changelings had sharp talon like claws as fingers. Some of them had thin patches of hair on their heads, while others were bald.

Simon stepped to the front of the group with a smug grin on his face. He was glad to see them all here because his plan had worked perfectly. The message he left had been received and now he could get what he really wanted. Melody focused on reading the room while Ezra stepped in front of her to block her off from anyone.

"Hello friends," Simon laughed, "It's so nice to see you all here. Now the fun can begin."

As he finished his sentence, five changelings with glowing yellow eyes threw themselves at Calpenitin and the fighters that stood closest to them. Spells were cast in the changelings' direction as they came at the army sending them through the air to land with a big thud overturning bookshelves and breaking tables. As soon as the first changelings hit the ground another group of them took their turn. This time Francesca and her fellow fighters took their turn at hand to hand combat. She quickly maneuvered out of the way dodging their attacks and throwing punches and kicks effortlessly. Francesca moved with great speed and agility taking out one after another. She was like an acrobat as she limbered through the air and landed graceful kicks knocking some unconscious and ending the lives of others using deadly force. Ezra watched fighters stabbing changelings causing black blood to spew and changelings clawing at fighters causing torn skin and blood loss as he continued to keep guard over his sister. Simon stood behind his minions for protection since he did not have any special ability of his own.

The dwarves joined the fight using their massive weapons and elves used their spells on the changelings that just kept appearing. There were fireballs and energy blasts all around. Calpenitin's attempts to wound Simon were useless. He was under some kind of protection that he just couldn't manage to break. As the battle inside the bookstore caused damage to the tables, bookshelves, and walls, the people walking on the street outside were completely oblivious to the magic and destruction of this epic battle going on inside.

In the heat of the fight, Ezra managed to get his hands on two changelings that came at him and Melody. He didn't have much training but it turns out all he needed was his brute strength. The changelings went down easily. It was almost as if they weren't really trying to hurt anyone. In the middle of celebrating his win, Ezra was caught off guard by another changeling. It came charging him quickly from the left side and he reacted at the last possible second. His instincts seemed to kick in when they were in trouble and without even knowing how, he shot the changeling with a giant fireball from his hand! The fireball flew from the center of his hand and hit the changeling at a great speed right in the chest. It was almost as if he planned it, but he hadn't. He had no idea how he did it and wasn't sure if he could even do it again.

"What was that?" Melody shouted over the noise.

"No clue," Ezra looked at his hands in disbelief and wondered what else he might be able to do.

With all the chaos of weapons clashing, spells crashing, and bodies dropping no one realized that Simon had disappeared until Calpenitin called their attention.

"You will not be victorious here today. Stand down and surrender. If not we will be forced to kill you all," Calpenitin addressed the remaining changelings.

Clearly, with Simon gone, they thought they had won the battle. But Melody quickly learned that they were up to far worse than they had originally suspected. She managed to read the thoughts of one of the changelings. She thought he seemed familiar and realized quickly that he was George Carson. She hadn't recognized him in his true form. But she recognized his thoughts. He was Simon's highest ranking man and he knew the real plan. A few managed to get away before the fighting ended, but most of Simon's changelings lay in puddles of black gunk on the floor around the book store.

Now that it was safe to move around the store, Melody quickly tried to explain what she had heard to the group,

"We aren't safe yet," she said while the group checked over the injured.

"Sir, I am afraid it is worse than we thought. I think this was all an elaborate hoax. Simon tricked us to bring us all here so that some dark wizard could get his hands on one of the pieces. I think it was all just a big distraction! We need to hurry back." Melody said.

Calpenitin led the group quickly back through the portal and toward the palace in Veya. They needed to treat their wounded and come up with a new plan. As soon as he arrived through the portal into Athelage he sent a message to Horen. He cast a spell and a cloud of smoke circled in front of him like a bubble to carry his message away. He needed to know if they had found any new information regarding the creation of the Peacekeeper that could be helpful. The keys to the cavern would probably be impossible to get ahold of and he wasn't even certain that there was a need to visit the cavern any more, but they needed to be prepared for Simon's next step. If he did, in fact, have a dark wizard working with him, he was much more dangerous than they had been giving him credit for.

"Sir Calpenitin, I am afraid we didn't find much that would be helpful. We managed to dig up an old journal that belonged to an apprentice. In it, he mentions keys to the wizard's cavern. There is also an old spell that maybe you can understand. It seems to be related to the keys, but we cannot decipher the meaning. We will bring it to the palace by morning." Calpenitin seemed interested to hear what they had found in Horen after all. They didn't realize how important this information might be when added to what they had already found in the bookstore. Calpenitin popped the bubble that floated in front of him which ended his conversation with the fighters' guild member in Horen. And they rode swiftly to the palace.

Chapter Thirteen: The Wizard's Quest

It was a rather spectacular scene to behold as the elves and dwarves joined by the wizard, magicians, fighters, and King and Queen entered the gates of the kingdom of Veya early that morning. The elves and dwarves had not been together in battle in over a thousand years, before the alliance of the Peacekeeper even. They had not had any common enemy since before the creation of the Peacekeeper. Wars had not been fought across Athelage since then. With the three kingdoms in an alliance, they did not have many enemies until now. It was like a parade of different regions riding through the town. The people stood on the streets watching and even cheered when they saw the King Morando, King Brovadan, and Queen Sephali. It wasn't every day this happened once let alone twice in as many days!

The palace was full of activity as a temporary infirmary was set up to take care of those that were injured. Tents were erected quickly within the palace courtyard to house the armies for the long haul. They didn't know what to expect next and the Kings agreed that it would be best to stay in Veya as they prepared for what would happen next. The palace staff returned to help prepare rooms for the visiting Kings and Queen. They were instructed to use discretion because they were sure to hear private conversations regarding the beginning war. The palace guards were recovering from their encounter with the enemy. Calpenitin worked to bring them back to full health while new guards were put in place. Prince Ezra, Princess Melody, King Brovadan and his most trusted council members of Warvelle, King Morando and Queen Sephali of Lauraan, Calpenitin, Kye, and Francesca all met in the war room to decide what their next steps would be. This was now the new Peacekeeper Alliance. They would help decide the fate of their world together and fight this enemy as one. But how would they fight this new enemy and keep Simon from the Peacekeeper?

As soon as the group was all together again in the palace with the apprentice's journal and the book from the store, Calpenitin worked quickly through the materials locked in a room undisturbed. He was starting to piece things together in order to tell the story of the wizard Walden and the Peacekeeper. Ezra and Melody waited anxiously as he worked through meals. Everyone else seemed to find things around the palace to keep them busy and distracted.

"Your Majesties, we have an urgent message from Warvelle in the library," a young female elf in a sheer green dress led Ezra and Melody quickly down the hall to a room just at the top of the main staircase.

The cozy library was filled with dwarves when they entered. They all sat silently with their heads bowed.

"What is it?" Ezra asked King Brovadan who stood at the center of the room with his people around him.

"Young prince, we are in mourning. We just received word that Warvelle was attacked. The piece that we kept so safe for all this time was taken. We also lost two good men."

Ezra put his hand on the King's shoulder to show his sympathy. He never felt like he knew how to comfort someone after they lost someone they cared about. He didn't have the words to make this better.

"So sorry for your loss, your majesty. But we will find him. And we will stop him!" Melody said. She sounded so sure that it was all going to work out and that they were going to be able to defeat Simon and his powerful wizard.

King Brovadan nodded in agreement and the silent dwarves in the room all raised their heads. And with just those words it was like they were awakened. The thought of avenging their loved ones was enough to get them back to work. And now they were all anxious to find out what Calpenitin was able to decipher from the journal. They didn't have to wait much longer to find out the details within those pages.

They all gathered together again in the large throne room and gave Calpenitin their full attention. He had spent the last eight hours scouring the books and putting together his version of the story. He thought he had a good idea of what Simon was up to and they needed to prepare a plan to stop him. He felt confident that now they had all the information.

"The great wizard Walden spent most of his life working in secret deep in the fairy woods. He had one apprentice, his daughter. She kept a journal that outlined spells and other magic objects he had created over that time. Walden was tired of all the war. He had lost so many people he loved that it had driven him to live in secret with his daughter. He was worried about her safety and wanted a new way of life for her future. This brought him to creating the Peacekeeper. Creating such a powerful object took everything out of him. This is why it took him so long to perfect it. She practically drew a map to the location because it was so detailed in her journal. And the best part of the whole thing, the picture of the keys he created that allowed only the two of them to enter the secret cavern. Walden hoped that the Peacekeeper would be unbreakable, but she was concerned about the safety of anyone who might try to destroy it. Destruction of the pieces would release all of the power they stored he assumed. This power would need somewhere to go. She wrote that the only way to destroy them would be in that same cave in that same underground pool where it was created. She seemed certain that destroying the Peacekeeper would create the most powerful being the realm had ever seen, even more powerful than her father. She tried to convince Walden not to finish the project because of the potential danger, but his desire for her to be safe in the world was just too much to argue against. When the Peacekeeper was complete Walden was completely drained of power."

"Simon would need to find the cavern to destroy the Peacekeeper and gain its power. Do you think he could do that?" Ezra asked when Calpenitin appeared to be finished with his story.

"But how do we find the cave and better yet how do we get in?" Melody added.

"It gets better," Calpenitin smiled at Ezra and paused for effect. "We already have the key." Calpenitin laughed while Ezra and Melody looked at each in confusion.

"What are you talking about?" Francesca stepped forward eager to hear more.

Calpenitin showed them the drawing from the journal. There, in faded ink, was a drawing of a beautiful glass doorknob, the same magical doorknob that Ezra now took out of his pocket. He turned it around in his hands and noticed the small details around the sides for the first time. Chiseled into the glass along the sides of the knob were vines wrapping all the way around. It was exactly like the drawing.

"How is that possible?" Ezra asked him.

The wizard shrugged his shoulders, "Just good luck, I suppose."

Almost immediately following Calpenitin's announcement the palace was full of activity once again. Everyone was back to work setting up or taking down. A group would set out for the fairy woods first thing in the morning, and there were so many things they needed to prepare before then. King Brovadan and King Morando would join Ezra, Melody, Kye, Calpenitin, and Francesca. Each dominion would bring one of their people on this quest while the rest stayed behind to guard the palace and treat the wounded. Queen Sephali would stay at the palace to oversee the guards and healers. Back in the war room staring at the map, Calpenitin used the descriptions written in the journal to mark out a route for them to follow to the fairy woods. King Brovadan rounded up weapons and put his men in charge of loading caravans with supplies for the journey. King Morando tended to the horses and checked in on the injured. Elves were known to be strong healers so he sent extra help to the makeshift infirmary. Kye rounded up the men and women who would be joining them on the quest and gave them their instructions. He was a good leader to his people and Ezra felt comfortable with him in charge of the soldiers. He looked up to Kye and hoped that one day he could lead his people in a similar way. Kye was straight forward and firm, but he cared deeply for everyone, no matter their dominion or title. When he spoke, everyone was listening.

"It will take us about two days to get to the fairy wood. And it will not be easy going. Be prepared. We all have something valuable to contribute and I hope that we will all be watching out for one another along the way. King Ezra and Queen Kasiah are depending on us here and I don't want to fail them. Some of us have been waiting our whole lives to make a difference like this and I hope we don't waste that chance. Some of us have hoped that something like this would never happen, but I am so proud of you all for being here anyway." Kye addressed the group.

"What do you know about the fairy wood?" Melody asked. She hadn't heard anything about fairies until now and didn't understand why Kye suspected they would have difficulty getting there.

"Princess Melody, I really only know what the legends say about the fairy wood. I have never been there and I don't know anyone who has.

It is far south from here. On foot, it would probably take us weeks to get there, but with magic, we can get there more quickly. There isn't any civilization that far south. It's believed to be overrun with changelings, ogres, and who knows what other evils we might run into. The fairies that inhabit the woods are tricksters. They like to keep to themselves and don't like to be bothered. It is possible that they will not like us being there either and might try to slow us down if they can."

"So you think we will find Simon and his dark wizard there?" Melody asked. Things had been moving so quickly she wasn't entirely certain what they planned to do when they made it to the fairy wood or what to expect would be there waiting for them.

"That is what we are hoping for. Without the key, he won't be able to enter the cave. We have to stop him before he can get his hands on it. It only makes sense that he would go there since he seems to know so much about the Peacekeeper, I am sure he knew where to go once he had the first piece. We will be there to stop him once and for all." Kye explained.

"What about King Ezra and Queen Kasiah? Or Sarah and Cooper?" Ezra asked.

"We are still hopeful for their safe return. There is no reason to believe otherwise." Francesca tried to reassure them.

Ezra and Melody found it hard to sleep that night. The anticipation of the journey to Fairy Wood kept them up tossing and turning in their beds wondering what to expect. When Melody did sleep, she dreamt of a beautiful but dangerous forest filled with giant magnolia trees. In all the beauty she could feel the danger all around them. She felt uneasy and even in her dream, she knew her traveling companions felt it too. But they were still up with the sun and ready to set out on their horses on the journey far south.

Riding at a magical speed, they flew through the meadow to the south of Veya and past the portal that would take them to the outer world. The fighters' guild led the pack. Horses pulled wagons filled with supplies behind the rest of the alliance members. They traveled a great distance in no time and by sunset Kye was ready to stop to set up camp. Next to a small lake, the group set up their tents and worked to get a fire started. Using magic helped them to create a large, upscale camp just for the night. There were two magic tents set up near the water, one for the men and one for the women. With the snap of the wand, the two giant tents were in place side by side, big enough to fit twenty people each. Inside the tents, were comfortable cots with plush pillows, a fire pit, a small table and chairs, and even a dressing area. A string of lights went up between the two tents providing more light for the deep darkness that only comes from being in the middle of nowhere. There were no lights from the city all the way out here, just the moon and stars. A young dwarf with a bushy black beard named Cyrus worked to get food cooking over the fire for their people.

As Melody finished eating the magically summoned, instead of caught, fish that had been cooked over the fire, she listened to the men around her tell stories that had been passed down from generations about the Fairy Wood.

"I heard that once a dwarf stumbled into the Fairy Wood completely by accident. Before he knew where he was those fairies had him in their sights. They tormented him all night with high pitched noises that made his ears bleed and made him hallucinate things he would never repeat."

"My great grandfather used to have these scars all over his arms and neck. When I asked my father about it, he said that he had made a trip to visit an elf and got lost in the Fairy Woods for days. When he returned home he was covered in tiny little teeth marks," one of the young fighters said.

Melody wondered if the stories were true or just fantasies turned into history after all this time. She wondered if it was filled with magnolia trees like the place she dreamed up. Even with all the tales, everyone seemed excited for the opportunity to venture into the Fairy Wood and see it with their own eyes. Melody saw Ezra's face on the other side of the giant fire. The dancing fire reflected in his bright eyes. He didn't seem worried by the stories. If anything, Melody thought Ezra seemed like he belonged there. This was his rightful place around the fire, sharing stories, and preparing for a battle.

All of the chatter was interrupted by a loud and terrifying rumble. It sounded like a violent storm was coming right for them. Everyone's eyes quickly went to the sky. Melody didn't know what they expected to see in the pitch black sky but there weren't any clouds to be seen. When the sound came again, but closer, Calpenitin was the only one who seemed to recognize it.

"Dragon,' he hollered. No one moved. No one ran to hide and take cover. No one grabbed a weapon or went on the defense. They just continued to stare into the empty sky in hopes they would see a dragon.

Melody's heart was beating in her throat. She was confused and went to Calpenitin.

"That was a dragon? Why aren't we running or something?" she shouted over the voices.

"It won't hurt us. Actually, they tend to keep their distance, and we are probably camping in the dragon's normal hunting grounds. They are big and loud, but they are not a danger to us." Calpenitin smiled and patted Melody's shoulder as he tried to comfort her.

It was strange having all of these ideas of what things were based on fairy tales and movies. A lot of those realities weren't the same. Learning that fairies were trouble and dragons were nothing to worry about was a little confusing. Ezra agreed it was difficult to wrap his head around when Melody told him what Calpenitin had said to her about the dragon. The dragon did decide to keep its distance just like the wizard said, and Melody felt a little disappointed that she didn't get to see a real dragon. She used the dressing area in the tent to change for bed and found a cot to sleep on. Melody thought she probably wouldn't get much sleep in this strange place, but she hoped she might dream of the place with the beautiful magnolia trees again.

After a full day of traveling, Ezra couldn't wait to lay down his head and sleep came much easier than the night before. Melody dreamed of all the places they had been and she dreamed of dragons flying above them as they slept. She could see their giant veiny wings that spanned the entire length of their camp. She dreamed of their scales like a snake but the size of shingles on a rooftop. Melody saw them clearly as they danced together in the sky overhead blocking out the moonlight and casting massive shadows over the tents where they all slept. It felt like they were there to protect them; these giant ancient creatures were watching over them in this far away camp.

At the first sign of morning, they all headed back out onto the faint dirt path through more meadows. The horses continued to gallop at high speeds toward their destination without stopping. Melody found that she had to stay focused on what was in front of them while riding on the back of the horse or she would get motion sickness seeing all of the trees and hills flying past. It was almost dizzying.

"Is that it ahead?" Ezra asked thinking the grove of trees coming quickly in front of them might be their destination.

"Not yet," Calpenitin checked his map with one hand to find where they were headed. "I believe this is the Gor Lagoon." Calpenitin halted his horse and the rest of the group stopped behind him. He looked around for only a moment before he ordered them to proceed with caution.

"The Gor Lagoon is said to be a pretty dangerous swamp actually," Kye told Ezra. Just inside the first few rows of tall trees, Ezra decided that Kye was probably right. The name lagoon gave a much prettier picture than what they were facing. This was definitely a swamp.

"Careful!" Francesca hollered back to the rest of the group. "We are likely to face alligators and other swamp creatures. Don't let them spook you off of your horse."

Ezra had never ridden a horse before now, and he wasn't exactly sure how he was supposed to keep the horse from getting scared by an alligator. But he tried his best to watch where the horse was going as he led it through the shallow, muddy water uncertain of what might be under the water. The next step could take them deeper or right into an alligator if he wasn't careful. Suddenly the horses began to panic. One by one they started snorting and braying and pacing backward. They were uneasy and that uneasiness spread like wildfire. The horse in front with Calpenitin on its back reared up tossing him into the mud and ran quickly out of site. The other horses started jumping up and neighing loudly as if they were communicating with each other about something. They formed a sort of half circle around Calpenitin now sitting in the mud but didn't move any closer.

"What do we do?" Francesca was brushing the side of her horses head and trying to calm it while she looked to the wizard for guidance.

He stood up from the mud looking around and scratching his head. It was clear Calpenitin didn't know what had happened to spook the horses but they weren't going to get them to move forward without figuring it out. He took a couple of steps forward and all of a sudden there were snapping alligators jumping out from the murky water all around them. One of the horses got bitten on the hind leg and cried out in pain. The group panicked and the horses all cried out loudly. Melody couldn't figure out who was injured and if their group was safe with all the noise. Kye and Calpenitin were quick to react. They pointed their wands at the alligators and with a short chant, the alligators stopped with their chomping and ran away.

King Morando hopped down from his horse and quickly healed the injured horse. "He will be fine. It was just a tiny nip." He said as he gently stroked the horse's mane. "Now let's find your horse, friend," King Morando certainly had a way with animals, Melody thought as he called sweetly to the missing horse. Calpenitin's white horse returned to them after a few minutes of calling. They made it through the rest of the swamp waters without any problems, but Melody knew the horses were still on edge. She could feel her horse's muscles tense under her legs. But she continued to praise the horse and pet the top of his head to help him relax.

Leaving the swamp, they started heading slightly west. Calpenitin said they would soon reach the Wastelands.

"What's that?"

"What we now call the Wastelands used to be a very rich and populated town. It was a sort of middle ground for people from all dominions and beings of all kinds. They had rich commerce and trading here until the fairies drove everyone away. Now it is just a deserted town. All that's left are the ruins of buildings and decaying roads from what I've heard. Most people don't travel this far south because of the fairies and tales of dragons. There just isn't any reason to come this way really."

Calpenitin liked to tell Ezra and Melody stories about Athelage just as much as they liked to hear them. They continued to tell stories about the Wastelands until they were close enough to see the dilapidated houses. The once paved roads leading through the town were covered in cracks filled with overgrown weeds. The houses they walked past looked ransacked and falling apart. There was nothing left of what was once the busiest town in the south except for some abandoned tires, scrap metal, and left behind junk. Melody even saw a handmade doll discarded.

"Keep your guard up," Kye instructed the group. Although the town look abandoned, Kye wasn't willing to bet on it. He believed there might be changelings or worse dwelling in the abandoned homes out of sight, taking advantage of the quiet. It was the perfect place for the outcasts to take up residence.

The group rode through the rugged streets single file watching the buildings on each side on high alert. Francesca held her wand in one hand and her horse's reins in the other followed by Ezra and Melody. Everyone was quiet, listening for any sounds of life inside the town. Ezra let out an audible sigh of relief as the neared the end of the town without any incidents. And they left the small abandoned town unharmed.

"It's not much farther now. We should start to see the tops of trees at the bottom of that hill there," Calpenitin pointed out into the distance.

The sun was starting to set as they started setting up their camp just outside of the Fairy Wood. Kye did not want to send them into the unknown in the dark. Everyone agreed it would be best to wait until morning to venture inside. The magical tents were placed about 50 yards away from a small opening in the magnolia trees of the Fairy Wood. It was beautiful how the tree branches wrapped around each other slightly creating an entryway. From this distance, they could see gold stones laid into the ground creating a path going into the woods.

A fire was started and food was prepared while the friends gathered around and rested. Everyone sat staring at the fire in silence caught up in their own thoughts. They had come this far into the unknown, but there was still so much ahead of them. None of them knew what to expect when they entered the Fairy Wood in the morning, and they could only guess what Simon had planned. Making it through the Fairy Wood would be a challenge alone and then they still had to stop Simon from carrying out his plan.

Melody stood looking into a pool of water. The moon from a small cave opening above reflected off the surface of the water. The center of the pool bubbled like the water was boiling. She saw her disheveled reflection staring back at her as she looked into the pool. Her brother stood next to her holding her hand. She hadn't realized he was there until she saw his reflection. His face looked battered and exhausted as they both stared into the water. The glowing moon on the water seemed to get brighter as they watched. They stood there like that watching the water bubble and boil until the glowing became so bright they could hardly stand to look into it any longer. Together, still hand in hand, they stepped away from the water and raised their hands over their eyes to shield them from the bright light. A burst of energy like an explosion sent them flying back and crashing to the dirt floor of the cavern and all the light disappeared. Melody, in a daze, pulled herself into a sitting position and failed when she tried to stand. Looking around, she saw Ezra still lying next to her. At first, they seemed to be alone in the room, and then she saw Simon standing in the pool. She panicked. Who was going to help Ezra? Was the piece of the Peacekeeper destroyed?

Chapter Fourteen: Fairies and Other Beasts Ahead

Calpenitin, Kye, and Francesca stood with Ezra and Melody at the entrance of the Fairy Wood. The gold stones on the dirt between the towering magnolia trees created a path brightly shining in the sun. The pale pink petals that fell from the magnolia blossoms were scattered all over the stones creating a beautiful contrast of light and dark. They would follow this path all the way to the center of the Fairy Wood until they ran right into the entrance of the Wizard Walden's cave hideaway, they thought.

"It shouldn't take us more than a couple of hours to get there now," Calpenitin guessed as he tried to make sense of an old map he carried. It was a map that been tucked away in the Horen library for hundreds of years. He believed that the big blob in the center of the woods would be the cave.

The group left their horses outside of the woods and decided to go the rest of the way on foot. They walked two by two through the entrance in silence. The elves were the only ones unimpressed by the size and beautiful color of the magnolia trees all around them. The aromatic magnolia blossoms were in bloom and the petals fell softly on the ground, the perfect petals touching them on their way to the earth. They hadn't made it very far inside the woods when Melody started to feel tired. She thought maybe she had just become too accustomed to riding on the back of a horse instead of using her legs to get where they were going.

"Man, I feel like I didn't sleep at all last night," Ezra said as he yawned and stretched.

Calpenitin stopped in front of him, ran his hand down his black beard and looked around quizzically, "You know, suddenly I do too."

"How do you feel?" Francesca asked Melody.

"I wasn't going to say anything, but I feel exhausted." Melody slumped onto the ground as soon as the words left her mouth. "I don't... think...I can," Melody struggled to keep her eyes open once she was sitting on the ground. "I need... a.. break.".

Ezra and Francesca rushed to Melody and tried to help her up as her eyes closed. They sat down next to her and tried to wake her, but they found themselves fighting to stay awake too. One by one they all sat down on the stone path or found themselves slumped against a magnolia tree struggling to stay awake the same way Melody did.

"The fairies...they must have..." Calpenitin couldn't finish his sentence.

Melody stood on the stone path now with her companions while Calpenitin checked his map again. Somehow they had gotten turned around. No one was sure where they were any longer, but it seemed like they had been going in the same direction for hours.

"Something isn't right," he said scratching his beard.

The others glanced over his shoulder to see what he saw. It was true. Nothing on the map resembled where ever they were now. In front of them, they saw a waterfall and a small lagoon that were not anywhere on the map.

"Did you hear that?" Francesca jumped back and drew her wand from her belt. No one else heard anything at first. They stood in silence waiting for something to happen. Slowly they all drew their wands or weapons and stood in a circle around the prince and princess. Ezra was offended that they all felt he needed protection like some damsel in distress. He had magic powers too. He could protect himself and his sister just fine, he thought.

Suddenly they all heard a loud thundering coming from the trees in the distance and getting closer. The sound was like trees crashing and snapping. The ground started to shake as whatever it was got near. Melody imagined the ogre they had faced before coming through those trees, but it was something else. She could tell it was something else entirely when she heard it roar.

They heard the sound just before the giant beast broke through the trees in front of them. Nearing the path in front of them was a goliath of a beast. Melody had no idea what she was staring at or what to do next. They all seemed frozen in fear or disbelief staring up nearly two stories at the mammoth-like beast. Its body was covered in long hair and its feet had talons as long as Ezra was tall.

"Wizard, what is this?" King Morando panicked. Everyone looked to Calpenitin unsure of what to do until King Brovadan made the first move.

Brovadan, King of the Dwarves, was known to have a quick temper. He wasn't one to wait around for instructions when facing some unknown beast. He was a man who took action in the face of a threat without putting much thought into it first. The short, stout dwarf spun in a circle where he stood gaining momentum and threw his mallet at the beast. It was a sight to see as the massive beast was struck by the mallet belonging to the tiny dwarf. It roared in anger and stomped its feet as the mallet struck it on the side and controlled by magic, turned around and returned to the King's hand. Brovadan readied to strike again as the beast roared and shook the ground with its giant feet.

Everyone readied to attack back as they scrambled to stay out from under the beasts wild feet. King Morando and Kye struck the beast in unison with blasts from their wands. Francesca used her ability to manipulate water to try to knock the beast over with water from the lagoon, but it wasn't quite strong enough. Calpenitin was working quietly on a spell while Ezra wished he could figure out how to control his newest fire power. The wizard mumbled under his breath and waved his hands around while the others continued to dodge the beast's feet and strike it where ever they could.

The giant wailed when King Morando struck it hard with a lightning spell. It charged back at him, lowering its face to the ground to attack. The teeth were almost as big as the talons protruding out of its mouth. Its face was flat with giant holes in the middle like nostrils. The similarity to a mammoth ended at its size and furry body. This face coming at them was terrifying. It snarled as it lunged and chopped its teeth at Morando. Calpenitin used all his might to cast a spell to stop the animal. The spell meant to freeze it, only slowed it down enough for the fighters to get a couple of good hits in as Morando rolled away from those vicious looking teeth. The beast was severely injured and seemed to be giving up. Melody still stood frozen. Her ability didn't seem to be of any use in a fight like this and she didn't know how she could help her friends. Ezra used his super strength to pull a small tree from the ground and he hurled it into the air and struck the slowing beast one last time before it gave up in defeat. As the animal lay down in the grass submitting to its enemy, it started to shimmer and then the mammoth sized beast disappeared from the woods. Everyone stared at the grass where the beast had laid, confused.

"What just happened?" Melody asked looking to Calpenitin for answers.

"I'm not sure, Princess. It must be some sort of fairy trick."

And before the group could decide what to do next, the petals from the trees above them began raining down on them. The soft pink petals were so thick in the air that it obscured their view momentarily. They couldn't see each other in front of them at all only pink petals falling through the air. When the last petals fell, they were all back in the woods where they had been so tired, they couldn't help but fall asleep. Slowly they rose from the ground and investigated where they now were.

"How are we back here?"

"Was that a dream?"

"Did you have the same dream?"

They all were full of questions about what just happened to them. But no one had any real answers. Calpenitin's best guess was that it was a trick to try to get them to turn back. The petals from the trees must have put them to sleep. They all had the same dream though. They were all faced with a giant enemy, and they came out victorious before waking up right back where it all started.

"Who knows how long we have been sleeping here, we should get moving fast to make up for the time we have lost," Kye said as they all gathered on the path together and headed in the direction they had been traveling, toward the center of the woods.

"Avoid the petals this time," Calpenitin said and they all agreed.

The trees overhead that had sheltered them from the sun most of the day made it very dark as soon as the sun started its descent. They hadn't reached the cave as quickly as they had expected thanks to their unplanned nap in the woods. But Calpenitin thought they were getting close. The magic orbs they brought with them in their packs now flew ahead of them lighting the path as the dark forest loomed all around them. The dark Fairy Wood was much scarier than the woods in the day. It seemed a whole new bunch of creatures came to life in the dark with all their sounds and movements in the trees. Melody found herself clenching Ezra by the wrist every time she heard a loud noise. They were all uneasy as they continued the path unknowing what was out there waiting or what the fairies might do next.

"Do you see that?" King Morando's companion elf had been relatively quiet up until now. He anxiously pointed into the darkness in front of them at the light in the distance. This did not help to ease their anxiety of the forest. Kye suspected they were walking right into another fairy trap, but Calpenitin convinced them that there was no other way to go but forward. Reluctantly, the group continued to follow him toward the light.

As they got closer to the light Ezra could see that it wasn't one light, but many tiny lights floating about six feet above the path in front of them. The details became clearer and the lights turned into tiny little bodies with wings glowing in the dark night.

"Fairies," Melody whispered. They all stopped and stared for a moment at the hoard of fairies in their way. Melody was astonished by their beauty. Their lights were all different colors ranging from pale blue to deep violet and even pink. They looked small and delicate, harmless even.

"Let me handle this," King Morando stepped toward the fairies. Fairies were distant relatives to the elves and once they all belonged to the same region. He felt confident that he could speak to them and they would let them pass. Kye was skeptical, but they all waited silently.

"Hello, friends. I am King Morando of Lauraan. We aren't here to do you any harm. Would you be so kind as to help us on our way?"

Ezra waited and watched but from where he stood he could not hear the fairies response. King Morando asked the fairies if they knew of the cave they were looking for. He complimented their home and was very gracious. And before they knew it the fairies parted and let them pass by. They were so bright it almost hurt to look at them. Melody squinted and tried to make out their shape through the glow. The fairies were the size of her hand. Their wings were twice the size of their shimmery bodies. Their skin was the source of the different color lights. Melody thought their skin looked like diamonds shining through the lights. They stared back at her as she passed and for some reason seemed amazed at the sight of her as well. Some of the fairies bowed their heads and Melody respectfully nodded back at them.

Once they were passed the fairies, Calpenitin led them quickly toward the cave. Melody suspected that the fairies had given him some valuable information because he seemed to be in a hurry now.

"Whoa, slow down," King Brovadan said as he struggled to keep up on his short legs.

"There isn't time to slow down. Didn't you hear?"

"No, we didn't hear anything," King Brovadan said as he looked to the rest of them. They all shook their heads because no one but Calpenitin had actually heard what the fairies had to say.

"Simon has already passed through here. We don't have any time to waste. The cave should be just around this next curve in the path. There, where that tree is," Calpenitin pointed 20 or so feet ahead of them into the darkness.

Through the trees, they couldn't see anything that lay ahead in the darkness. Ezra was nervous about stumbling into Simon unprepared but Calpenitin would not slow down. Kye told the group to get ready. King Morando drew his shiny silver wand from a leather pouch hanging from his waist. Francesca pulled her pony tail tight and readied her wand. King Brovadan kissed his weapon for luck and nodded to Kye showing he was ready. And they all picked up their pace to keep up with the wizard. Melody felt her heart beating so hard in her chest that she thought it might just jump right out of her throat, and Ezra felt like he had a watermelon in his stomach and he might be sick as they got closer to the cave. But he took a deep breath and tried to shake out the nerves before the cave was in sight.

None of them knew what to expect as they neared the entrance to the cave. But there it was, almost hidden by overgrown grass and weeds as tall as Melody. The rock jutted out from the side of a hill. And there in the center was a dark wood door a small hole in the center underneath a gold image of the Peacekeeper. Ezra remembered seeing the image in a book. It was round with zigzag lines through it separating the whole into three pieces. Each piece marked with a unique symbol representing the dominion it now belonged to. It looked similar to a best friends necklace that Melody once owed with its puzzle piece type cuts dividing it equally for three. Calpenitin rubbed his hand over the symbol on the door as he soaked in every inch of it. He couldn't believe that they were here where the Peacekeeper had been created all those years before his time by the Great Walden. It would have been a dream come true under much different circumstances.

132

"Ezra, do you have the key?" Calpenitin reached his hand out and motioned to Ezra. He stepped toward the wizard as he pulled the seemingly normal glass doorknob from his pocket. He turned it over in his hands once and said a silent prayer that this would really work before he placed the small end of the knob into the hole. Ezra quickly turned the doorknob that was now inside the hole in the middle of the cave door and felt it click as it caught the lock of the door before the door opened for them. Everyone huddled around trying to get a look inside as soon as the door opened.

Inside the cave was dark and dank, much like a cave would be. It didn't seem like anything special at first. Calpenitin took a step inside and with a flip of his wand lit up a row of lanterns hanging on the right side of the wall. Cautiously, the group entered the cave one by one following the row of lanterns inside. Their feet were quiet on the dirt floor as they went. They had expected to find Simon trying to enter the cave when they arrived, but since they did not see him, Francesca closed the door tight behind them to keep him out. She wasn't sure what the plan was now that they were inside with the door locked shut but she followed behind the others deeper into the cavern. Ezra could feel everyone's anticipation at seeing what lay inside the cave. They had only imagined what it might have been like to create such power in the Peacekeeper but now they would get to see where it was made all those years ago.

Roughly ten yards in and they entered a giant room. The room still looked like someone's home. There were rows and rows of brightly colored books along the walls collecting dust. Ezra saw a table with two chairs made of wood next to a fireplace in one corner. In the farthest corners of the room opposite each other were two small beds and two small dressers. There was even a floor length mirror hung between what looked like two distinct and separate sleeping areas. Ezra wiped his finger in the thick layer of dust on the large oak desk near the entrance of the room. Everything seemed to be covered in it. The group investigated the room in silence taking it all in for a moment.

"Look here," Melody pointed to a giant stone that looked like it was covering an opening in the wall at the back of the room near one of the beds.

"I guess we should go this way," Kye said as he placed a book back on the shelf and followed Melody.

Ezra used all his might to roll the stone away from the opening and they all went through together with apprehension. Melody could feel her heart racing in her chest again, uncertain what might be on the other side. She envied Ezra and all of his strength. He was so powerful and so confident in his new ability. Ezra didn't seem to be scared of anything anymore. As they entered the next chamber of the cave, she remembered her recent dream. Here they were standing in a large cave and not far in front of them was the same large pool of water that she had dreamed of. The moon peeped through a hole in the ceiling of the cave and reflected off the water just like in her dream. Water dripped steadily from the stalagmites that hung down over the pool. Melody's heart pounded so loudly she could hardly hear anything over it but the sound of King Brovadan's heavy breathing behind her. King Brovadan, King Morando, the wizard, Kye, Francesca, Melody, Ezra, the dwarf Cyrus and the elf named Winn stood staring into the cave opening each waiting for someone else to make the first move inside.

The silence was suddenly broken by the sound of voices back inside the old wizards living quarters. The group all heard it and jumped away from the opening in the cave wall. Kye stood in front of the princess and pulled out his wand. King Brovadan raised his weapon and jumped next to Kye in order to shelter the children. Melody was getting a little tired of being treated like she was so fragile.

"Just wait," Calpenitin put his arm out to stop Francesca as she neared the opening.

Melody knew who was coming and they were about to be face to face with their enemy and his band of misfit souls. She could tell the others knew it too by the determined looks on all of their faces. This was what they had come for. They were ready to end this all now. Calpenitin had ordered them to wait for the enemy to come to them so they backed slowly away from the opening and closer to the edge of the pool.

"Mel, look," Ezra pointed to her necklace. The gold charm was glowing bright like it had before. The light from the necklace flashed for a few seconds almost like it was warning them.

Melody could feel them before she could actually hear their thoughts. And when the thoughts became audible in her head she knew more of Simons plan. They had been on the right track all along. He was here to destroy the part of the Peacekeeper and gain power again. And the dark wizard would help him do it. His army of changelings had been severely depleted during their last encounter, but he was still very confident that nothing was going to stop him here. And he was actually hoping that Ezra and Melody would show up to try to stop him. His dark thoughts of torture and domination made Melody's stomach turn.

"Well isn't this a wonderful surprise?" Simon clapped his hands together and smiled when he finally entered the room. "It's the weary old wizard and his crew. I had small hope that you would find out what that doorknob could really do but I didn't think you would beat me to it," Simon said as he tossed a matching doorknob back and forth between his two hands.

That was the plan all along. Simon had his own doorknob and Calpenitin was frustrated that he had not considered that maybe the second key was around somewhere. Calpenitin made the first move. He raised his wand and shot a bolt of lightning in Simon's direction, but he appeared to still be under some form of magical protection. Simon laughed at Calpenitin's attempt and his dark wizard friend stepped forward to stand beside him.

"Take care of this. I have important things to do here," Simon said to him.

The dark wizard with the hood of his robe pulled up over his face nodded his head and stepped closer to them. He was tall and very thin. His dingy black robe dragged across the floor as if he was floating under it. His face was well hidden and his hands were covered by the hanging sleeves. The changelings gathered behind him ready to assist. The dark wizard then raised his left hand toward Calpenitin. His fingers were boney and the skin was gray. He aimed his finger like a gun and they were all struck by an invisible force almost like an explosion. It sent them flying back against the rock wall of the cave and to the ground. Francesca tried to stand but the explosion had caused rocks to tumble down on her, pinning her legs. Ezra quickly went to her aid and they charged back at the enemy. Again and again, he struck them with a magical force so strong, Calpenitin couldn't compete. Morando sent spells and Kye tried to rush him, but they just couldn't get close enough to do any damage to the dark wizard. He was just too powerful for them to beat.

While the group was distracted by the dark wizard, Simon made his way to the pool of water. He took the piece of ancient metal that came from the Peacekeeper from his pocket and stepped into the water. It was shiny gold and shaped like a piece from a puzzle. Similar to the charms Ezra and Melody wore, it was covered in intricate cut out designs.

"Ezra!" Melody tried to get his attention as she watched helplessly. She was no match for Simon or the dark wizard but she knew that they had very little time to stop what was going to happen. Simon was determined to complete the ritual and he knew that his dark wizard was unstoppable. He was confident and excited as he entered the water and raised the piece up into the moonlight.

As the group realized what was happening, they tried to split up in order to keep the wizard busy and stop Simon, but the dark wizard saw it coming. His boney fingers reached out toward Brovadan, Kye, and Cyrus as they attempted to reach Simon. He placed a powerful spell on them all with a flick of the wrist that stopped them in their tracks. They couldn't move a muscle. Brovadan, Morando, Calpenitin, Kye, Francesca, Melody, Ezra, and the others were paralyzed. They couldn't even speak a word. But Melody could still read their minds, all but the dark wizard. His mind seemed to be as strong as he was. With Ezra, Melody and their friends stuck, the dark wizard joined Simon in the center of the pool to complete the ritual.

They held the piece of the Peacekeeper up into the air together. It had rugged edges and was the size of Simon's hand. Together they chanted. The chanting became louder as the changelings joined in around the outside of the pool. The bright moon shined on the metal and it began to glow. There was excitement on the grotesque faces of the changelings as they saw what was about to happen. The light from the piece grew brighter and brighter. It hurt Melody's eyes to look at it. Ezra tried to turn away but all he could do to protect his eyes was close them. The light became so intense that even Simon couldn't look at it anymore.

Melody caught a glimpse of their reflection in the water just before there was a giant explosion and the entire cave shuddered. Rocks went flying and everything went black for a moment. Melody panicked and realized she could move again. She had been shaken from the spell or it had worn off and she was now free to move around. But she couldn't see. She crawled around on her hands and knees reaching out for her brother. She knew that he had been right beside her before the blast.

"Ezra?" she called as she used her mind to try to feel for his presence.

"Here. I'm here," he grabbed her arm and helped her to stand.

"Ez, I can't see anything. Why is it so dark?" As soon as the words came out of her mouth she felt her brother's panic. It wasn't dark, it was just her, she couldn't see!

"Oh no, Ezra! Why can't I see anything?"

Melody felt soft hands cover her eyes for a moment and when they were removed she could see again. King Morando stood in front of her now after healing her sight and checked her over for any other injuries. Everyone was circled around her and seemed uninjured but looked a little battered from the explosion.

As soon as he knew his sister was going to be okay, Ezra turned his attention back to Simon. The dark wizard had vanished but Simon was lying on the dirt ground next to the pool unconscious from the blast like many of his changelings. Ezra and Kye approached the pool cautiously. The changelings that were left standing didn't put up a fight. They decided to flee with their wounde. Ezra used the tip of his foot to shake Simon. He didn't look dead.

"Where are my parents and the King and Queen?" Ezra yelled as he tried to wake Simon.

His eyes opened and he glared at Ezra. Calpenitin pushed Simon and Kye back away from Simon as he got to his feet. Melody could tell he was worried. There was no way to know if he had completed his ritual. And if he had, they didn't know what kind of power he might possess. Simon didn't know if it had worked either. Melody heard his thoughts churning away. All he wanted was to get out of there and recover from the blast. He needed time to figure out just how to use whatever power he now had. And he needed to meet up with his dark wizard friend. And just like that, he disappeared.

"What just happened?" Ezra looked to Kye and Calpenitin for an answer, but they were surprised too.

"Wait, I know where they took Mom and Dad!" Melody said. She had seen it in Simon's mind when Ezra asked him about them. And she recognized the place. It took her a moment to remember where she had seen the dilapidated house and the large faded billboard. But when she remembered, there was no denying it.

"They are in the Wastelands."

"Let's go!"

Chapter Fifteen: This is Not the End

They didn't waste any time getting to the Wastelands, the once bustling city now abandoned. Since Melody knew where they were going she used the magic doorknob to take them to the street just in front of the empty house she had seen in Simon's mind. It was still dark out as they stepped through the door tired and banged up. Melody stood in the street where they had arrived and looked up at the houses in her view. Even in the dark, she knew this was it. She pointed it out and they quietly checked the windows to see if anyone was inside. Melody cast her mind out toward the beat up shack that stood in front of her with her hand on the brass doorknob. She could barely feel them, but she knew that her parents were inside.

"I think there might be just a couple changelings in there with them. I don't hear much," she whispered.

Kye nodded to Ezra giving him the signal he needed to break the door down and they rushed inside before the changelings had a chance to react. Calpenitin and King Morando cast spells quickly taking out the off guard changelings. And the rest scrambled through the two-story house searching for the prisoners.

"Down here," Francesca hollered from the basement stairs. Ezra and Melody looked at each other with hopeful smiles as they rushed to meet Francesca. Ezra took the stairs two at a time and saw them first. Sarah and Cooper were chained to the wall next to King Ezra and Queen Kasiah locked up in a cell similar to the one that Ezra and Melody had been held in. Much to their surprise, Melody's singing instructor, Ms Capechio was locked in the cell too. Francesca worked to pick the lock of the magic cell while Ezra and Melody tried the cuffs on Sarah and Cooper.

"Our babies! I am so glad you are okay. You are okay aren't you?" Sarah tried to embrace her children and inspect them for injuries but they didn't have time to waste. If this was Simon's safe house, he could come back at any moment.

Quickly the group exited the basement and collectively used the magic doorway to head back to the castle where they would be safe. Once they were in the safety of the war room they could figure things out.

The king and queen gave Sarah and Cooper a moment alone with their children before they got a chance to talk.

"Mom, are you okay?" Melody hugged her mom close and didn't want to let go. She couldn't believe that she was here now and Sarah felt the same. She wasn't sure she would ever see the kids again, but they had saved her. She was so proud of them. Melody stroked her auburn hair and took in her familiar smell. Sarah did the same. After a long hug, she pulled Melody away so she could look her over. In the week since she had seen her, she felt Melody had grown so much. She had matured. The experiences she had in Athelage had grown her in a way that Sarah couldn't imagine. She smoothed Melody's blonde hair behind her ear and kissed her forehead. Cooper pulled them all into a group hug after Ezra checked him over. The last time they had seen him, in the office at their house, there had been so much blood. Ezra had tried to stay hopeful for his sister's sake, but he didn't really think that Cooper had made it.

King Ezra and the rest of the alliance entered the war room again. They needed to fill in the king and queen and decide what they would do next. Calpenitin and King Morando filled everyone in on what had happened in the fairy wood. They weren't sure that Simon had been successful with his task, but Calpenitin suspected it had worked. It was only a matter of time before he tried to use his powers or take another piece of the Peackeper for himself. He wouldn't be satisfied with just a little power now that he had it. As the sun began to rise, they decided to get some rest before they decided anything. King Ezra made sure his guard was strong and ready for Simon before he took to his chambers.

As all the arrangements were being made and everyone was settling in, Ezra and Melody had time to sit down with Sarah and Cooper.

"What happened that night?"

"Where were you being kept that whole time?" Melody and Ezra questioned them. They wanted to know every detail. Anything big or small might be able to help them.

"Are you okay?" Melody looked to Cooper specifically when she asked.

"Slow down you two. We are okay. I am so sorry that you were worried about us and that you had to go through all of this without us. I hoped that we would be able to tell you about Veya one day. We never expected for you to find out about it the way you did," Sarah answered.

"We trusted Simon wrongly. I can't believe we put you in this danger, to begin with," Cooper added.

Melody could tell that they were upset at themselves for what happened. But there was no way they could have known better. Simon had fooled everyone all of this time.

"The changelings took us to the house and kept us there. It wasn't that bad. We were just worried about you two especially after the king and queen arrived." Sarah swept Melody's hair out of her face and smiled. She was trying to make her feel better. Melody smiled back, but she didn't feel like smiling. "You were so brave." Sarah told her.

"They brought us to the bookstore one night and made your mother share everything she knew about the Peacekeeper. We had no idea that Simon could do something like this. We didn't even know he was involved with those changelings until he showed up with the King and Queen. How could he?" Cooper shook his head.

"I wish we had some of our things," Sarah said as she looked at her filthy clothes and hair in the reflection of a mirror in the sitting room. She would feel much better after a shower and a change of clothes. Cooper agreed it might be nice to have their own things.

Ezra was worried about them leaving the protection of the palace full of trained fighters and magicians, but he understood that they felt very out of place and had been through so much. Having a few of their own things might make them feel more at ease, so he suggested to the Alliance council that he and Melody accompany them and maybe Kye and Francesca could come along just in case. King Ezra and Queen Kasiah seemed the most concerned with this idea. After being apart from their children all this time, they were anxious to have them leave. But Kye assured them that these kids were tough and had shown amazing strength mentally and physically. Francesca promised they would be safe, and everyone there was inclined to believe her because she had done so much to protect them this far. It was decided that they would make a quick trip. With permission from the rest of the council, Calpenitin would open a new portal. This was typically not allowed because it was dangerous. King Ezra had banned most of the portals for their safety many years ago, but this exception would make for safer travel in this specific situation. The portal would take them directly from the palace to the house.

Kye, Francesca, Ezra, and Melody would travel with them as a precaution. Melody was eager to have some of her own things as well so she could change out of these black fighter's clothes she had been wearing. Ezra thought they were cool though. He felt like he belonged with the group in his black pants and black hooded shirt and weapons belt. He could easily maneuver in the clothes and they were so lightweight he felt like he wasn't wearing anything at all. He felt like a real-life ninja sneaking around in all black. And he was ready to fight if he had to. If he wasn't already a prince, he would want to be a fighter.

The portal was open and they all went through quickly. Melody thought she might never get used to that feeling of being magically transported from one place to another; her stomach jumping into her throat as they traveled between realms. Sarah seemed to feel the same by the look on her face when she was standing in their living room again.

"It certainly looks like the scene of a crime in here, huh?" she said as she noticed the broken furniture and the papers scattered everywhere. She put her arm around Melody and hugged her close to her side. After all these years of protecting her from something like this, she was hurting thinking about all her children had now seen. She wished she could have prepared them for what happened. But she was also so very proud of them. It was almost like they had grown five years since she saw them. Melody and Sarah walked together to the upstairs of the house to gather some things from their rooms. Kye walked around the house checking out the rooms while Francesca stayed close behind Sarah and Melody. Cooper and Ezra made an attempt to clean up. They picked up broken objects and stuffing that now littered the floor and put it in the trash. Cooper swept up glass from a broken picture frame and Ezra piled up papers in a nice stack unsure of what might be salvaged.

"Ready?" Cooper asked when Sarah and Melody returned to the living room each carrying a small duffle bag of their belongings.

"Let's get out of here. It just doesn't feel like home anymore," Sarah said.

"Agreed," Cooper hugged her and kissed her forehead.

Ezra and Melody didn't think the house felt the same either. All of the good memories they shared in this house like Christmas mornings and movie nights had been overshadowed by the one very terrible thing that happened there. For days they thought their father had died in that office at the hands of a monster they did not see. Someone had gone through their things and torn apart their life. The house was not home after being invaded and ripped apart.

As they all prepared to go back through the portal to Veya, Kye stopped suddenly and reached out his arm toward them. He placed his finger over his mouth to signal for them to be quiet. Ezra's heart began to race. He thought he heard something too. Kye signaled something to Francesca. She nodded and crept over toward them. Kye silently moved toward the stairs listening for any noise. But they didn't hear anything else. Hearts racing, adrenaline pumping, and fear sinking in they all watched Kye and Francesca for some sign of what to do next. Melody wasn't sure what was happening so out of instinct she tried to read the room. Kye had definitely heard something upstairs. He thought someone was up there and was worried if they went through the portal whoever it was might follow behind them. He needed to see who it was and take care of it before anyone went through the portal. Frantically Melody tried to listen for unwanted guests. Her family was all stressed and their thoughts were flying at her left and right making it harder for her to focus. Just as she was able to read that there was, in fact, someone upstairs, that person came charging at Kye on the stairs. Kye and the mysterious person tumbled down the stairs in a blur each fighting to land on top. It happened so quickly no one else had time to react. When they landed at the bottom of the stairs, Kye was on top of a wild changeling. He pinned her arms to keep her from clawing at him as Francesca rushed up the stairs to check for anyone else.

"Who else is up there?" Kye yelled at the changeling under him. She didn't say a word as she squirmed and fought to try to get out from under him so she could rip him to shreds.

And then there was a crash upstairs and Francesca yelled. Kye quickly drew his wand from his weapons belt and cast a spell on the changeling rendering her unconscious, and he raced up the stairs to join his sister. Melody yelled for him to stop, but he didn't listen. It was a trap. Up the stairs and to the right Simon and his dark wizard now held Francesca. She was pinned to the wall using magic that Simon now possessed. Melody knew all of this before Kye went up the stairs, but she didn't have a chance to warn him.

"It's Simon! And he has powers!" she frantically explained to Ezra.

Everything happened so quickly after that. Ezra sent Sarah and Cooper back through the portal to keep them safe from harm before Simon and his wizard friend came down the stairs to stand in the living room right in front of Ezra and Melody. The dark wizard stood behind Simon nearly seven foot tall. He wore the same long black robe with a hood covering his face. He was quietly chanting a spell of some kind with his shiny silver wand extended toward them in his boney hand.

"It's so good to see you two again," Simon smiled.

"What do you want from us?" Ezra shouted at him.

"Hasn't Melody already figured that out for you all?" he chuckled but didn't really give them a chance to respond before he continued. "I want to right the wrong that was done to me all those years ago. I will gain back my full power. I will gain all of the power. No one can stop me now!"

"We will stop you!" Ezra replied. He was certain that Simon wasn't going to be able to do what he set out to do. They had an army and he had a group of changelings that were quickly being taken out.

"Always were a little full of yourself Ezra. Or should I say, Prince Ezra?" Simon was smug. He stepped closer to them laughing as if he had already won.

Ezra charged at him and attempted to pin him but the wizard that had been standing there silently used his magic to quickly pull Ezra away. He threw Ezra to the wall causing him to hit his head and go limp to the floor. Melody panicked. She didn't have super strength or some magic wand to cast great spells of protection. She wasn't even sure she could fully control her natural power yet. Her greatest allies, Kye and Francesca, were unconscious or under some sort of spell upstairs and she was face to face with the enemy, all alone. Not to mention she was the only thing now standing between Simon and the portal straight into the palace. She could wait in hopes that Sarah and Cooper could send help through or she could take action.

She was angry. She balled up her fists and thought of all the things she wanted to do to Simon and all the things he had done to hurt her and her family. He wasn't going to get away with this. This wasn't the way this ended.

"Awe, is the princess upset?" Simon mocked her. This only made her angrier.

And suddenly without any thought or intent Melody raised her hands and blasted Simon and the dark wizard with an invisible force more powerful than anything she had ever seen. Their limp bodies flew through the air contorted by the blast. She heard the sound of breaking bones and tearing muscle as they were thrown through the exterior wall of the home. Stunned, she stood there for a moment before rushing over to check on Ezra. She got him to his feet just as Kye and Francesca came bolting down the stairs, weapons ready. At that same exact moment, four fighters that looked like they had been awakened from their sleep stepped through the portal with their wands in the air. Melody didn't know what to say so she just pointed in the direction she had thrown Simon moments ago. The fighters ran in the direction and stepped through the hole that was now in the side of the house. Francesca and Kye came to check on Ezra as he held his throbbing head.

"What happened?" Francesca asked.

"I don't know," Melody wasn't sure how to explain what just happened or what that new power was, but it was likely it saved them all today.

The fighters returned to the house empty-handed and confused. Simon and his dark wizard had vanished. They had gotten away, but it was safe to say they were badly injured by Melody's blast.

"Let's get out of here," Kye was anxious to get everyone back to safety.

Once they were all through the portal and Calpenitin sealed it up tight, Melody explained to them what had happened and Francesca filled in where she could. Everyone was stunned that Melody had demonstrated such strong magic. Even she couldn't believe it happened. It seemed Ezra and Melody each possessed more power than anyone had realized.

The war with Simon was only just beginning, but there was a new sense of peace in the realm. King Ezra and Queen Kasiah were finally reunited with their children. They now knew the enemy that they were facing and just what he was capable of doing. King Ezra planned the biggest celebration in Veya since the day he was married. He was excited to officially welcome his children back properly and show them off to his people. It would be nice for the different people of Athelage to come together and have something to celebrate after all that had happened and what they were about to face together.

King Ezra stood on a raised platform behind a long table in the grand ballroom of the palace wearing his nicest white suit. His gold crown looked like two dragons entwined around his head. Queen Kasiah was seated at the table by his side in a flowy deep purple dress.

"Ladies and gentlemen, I am so happy to have you all here with us tonight to celebrate. And what a joyous celebration," he smiled from ear to ear and his gray eyes shined under the bright lights.

"I am so proud to introduce Prince Ezra Ezeen VII and Princess Melody Estelle," King Ezra turned his attention to the other end of the ballroom where the enormous double oak doors were being opened by two guards.

Ezra and Melody stood on the other side of the doors hand in hand. Ezra was dressed like a real prince. He wore a suit similar to his father's with deep purple trim. He wore a small gold crown fixed with small purple gemstones on his head. His sister wore a dress fit for a princess. She was dressed in purple tulle and lace, her dainty gold crown on her head. Melody finally felt like a real princess at this moment. The crowd of people from all over Athelage applauded for them as the doors opened and even bowed for them as they entered the room. They entered the grand ballroom with the shiny white marble floors and gilded everything and joined their parents at the long table.

As soon as everyone had finished eating, they were anxious to get a chance to talk with the prince and princess. A band played music and people started dancing in the space in the middle of the room. There was laughter and conversation all around the room. Everyone was dressed up and enjoying themselves, even the fighters of Horen found it appropriate to relax a little during this celebration. The party went on long into the night. Calpenitin, however, stayed seated in his place at the table with the King and Queen.

"What do we do now?" Melody asked Calpenitin.

"Now, we rest. Then we prepare to protect the other pieces with everything we have. Plus we need to get you both some magic training! You both are made of some serious powerful stuff, dear Princess. And we plan to teach you how to harness and control all that power!"

Made in the USA
Las Vegas, NV
24 August 2021